Walk Me Through the Haze

Walk Me #2

Nicole Dennis

Blurb

Getting the hell out of Texas and an abusive relationship, Doctor Evan Sampson drove away without looking back, taking a chance with his uncle's clinic in small-town Montana. He can only hope things go better for him – professional and personal.

Ending a successful tour run with the band, Joshua Holmwood tries to conceal the pain in his wrist from his 'brothers'. It doesn't work and he accepts how he needs a doctor.

Upon reaching the ranch, coming home isn't all fun and games for the guys. While Sage receives bad news from the new doctor, Josh learns there is more to his injured wrist. At the same time, he doesn't conceal his interest from the doctor, who returns the same. When his injury turns tenfold, Doc Evan is again by his side. Josh hopes they can go from a patient-to-doctor relationship to a lover-to-lover one.

Warning: Abuse, medical stuff, a steamy doctor, and a cowboy who doesn't give up — even while being a cranky toddler.

FatCat Books Ink

Trademarks

The author acknowledges the trademarked status and owners of the following word marks used in this story:

Jeep Compass: *Chrysler Group LLC*

Porsche: *Porsche USA*

BMW: *German BMW Group Holdings Limited*

M&Ms: *Mars, Incorporated*

iPod: *Apple, Inc.*

Motel 6: *The Blackstone Group*

iTunes: *Apple, Inc.*

Stetson: *John B Stetson Company*

Cheetos: *Frito-Lay North America, Inc.*

Glacier National Park: *U.S. National Park Service*

Ford F-150: *Ford Motor Company*

Jell-O: *Kraft Heinz*

Mary Poppins: *Disney Enterprises, Inc*

• • • •

Chapter One

Squeezing the handle, topping off the tank of the three-year old Jeep Compass, Evan Sampson watched the numbers roll across the small screen. He dropped the little lever to hold the handle and let the pump do its job. He glanced around the station but didn't see the silver Porsche anywhere. Instead, the latest Texas heat wave rose from the hood in a shimmering pattern. He wove his fingers through the pattern, watching it change and bend. This would be his last Texas heat wave. His final destination was far from here.

He tugged out the golden necklace and kissed the rainbow cross. Letting it fall, he kept it close and hoped it brought him strength and comfort. He couldn't drop his determination and decision. He touched the small scratch on his cheekbone, surrounded by a swollen bruise.

There was no going back.

This was it.

Back in the fake perfect house, which held all kinds of secrets and lies, he knew George Anderson, someone he once thought he loved, would be rolling on his back, snoring loudly. Thanks to all the liquor he poured down his gullet, he wouldn't wake up anytime soon. There were no more second chances. George had cracked the back of his hand against his face last night.

Evan couldn't believe he fell for the bastard's routine, again.

He was done. He wouldn't take the lies. He wouldn't take the abuse.

George went beyond the physical, mental, and verbal. He kept up the constant pressure of Evan moving beyond working in the ER to a more prestigious position. He badgered and yelled when Evan turned in his older model Jeep to purchase the Compass instead of a high-end car. George wanted Evan to get a BMW convertible like other doctors. He wanted it to match the Porsche he'd splurged on for no reason other than the damn name. Either way, George wanted to drive around to all the parties and get-togethers he insisted on attending like a proper couple. Evan hated those stuffy parties. After long difficult shifts, he preferred relaxing with a glass of wine and a good book. George forced him to dress in attire he wanted and shoved him out the door to yet another dinner or party. If he didn't attend or behave in a certain way, portraying George as a brilliant surgeon and doting partner, there were consequences. They left Evan in hours of pain.

Screw the damn parties. Forget the abuse where George felt far superior for being a surgeon. Evan was a fucking accomplished doctor in his own terms, even if he didn't go into surgery. He received notoriety and awards for his work in the ER and other clinics.

Hell, he knew better than to stay in any type of an abusive relationship. He saw the results of victims moving through the ER. He took care of them, knowing he could be the next patient in that bed.

How fucked up was he to stay with a drunk bastard like George Anderson?

While George had been on his latest rotation, Evan took the chance to pack most of his belongings and store them in an unused room. As soon as they got home from the party and George went to the bedroom, Evan shoved all those boxes into the Compass. There were some items he couldn't pack since George could figure out what was happening. He had to wait until the last minute. Grabbing the last three suitcases, he yanked and shoved his clothes from the closet and dresser drawers into the cases. He scooped and dumped his toiletry items into another bag. Every once in a while, he stopped when he heard George grumbling and shifting in the bed. With the amount of liquor in him, George never opened his eyes.

Carrying the last suitcases to the car, he paused and collected some of the last-minute personal items which mingled within George's stuff. Knowing he couldn't leave some of his favorite books, he grabbed a flattened box he left in the garage, folded it while he walked, and entered the small library-office. He boxed his favorite books and trinkets. Covering the box and lifting it, he went through the house a final time as he returned to the garage. Pushing the box into the Compass, he closed the back. Going through the key ring, he removed the house keys and mailbox key. He tossed them onto the kitchen floor.

Climbing into the Compass, he pulled out of the garage, closed the door with the opener. After the door closed, he tugged the opener free from the visor, opened the window, and tossed the opener toward the garden by the front door. He couldn't give a shit where it landed.

Flinging his middle finger at the door and the man inside, he drove away from the rest of the *perfect life* he left behind. He would let the bastard rot in bed. Evan wouldn't be there to offer any more excuses to the hospital for the delays of attending a surgery or meeting. He wasn't covering for the bastard any longer.

If the hospital fired George from his so-called "prestigious position," it was his own damn fault.

Evan wouldn't be around to take the fall or abuse. Desperate to keep everything quiet and hidden from George, he didn't resign from the position at the hospital. He couldn't, since the damn rumor mill would get to George, who would throw a temper tantrum — taking it all out on Evan. Nope. This way was the best. He had to leave quick and fast. He would deal with the hospital later. Much *much* later.

Hell, fucking no would he let George find him. He would be more than fifteen hundred miles away.

He planned on enjoying a completely different life. He willingly left working at a busy Dallas ER to become a quiet country doctor. Taking the chance, he accepted the offer from his uncle, a family member he never talked to George about, not that he gave a damn about Evan's family.

Hearing the old gas pump shut off, Evan replaced the handle. Thanks to the age of the station, he needed to pay inside. He strolled through the double glass doors, ignoring the occasional stare when others caught the noticeable bruise. Heading through the grocery area, he tugged out multiple bottles of cold water, different options of salty snacks, four bags of M&Ms, and stopped at the coffee counter. He poured black coffee into the largest cup they had and fixed it with a touch of cream. Juggling everything, he made his way to the register.

"Topped off on pump three and all this," Evan said as he laid everything across the counter.

"Going on a trip?"

"A permanent one," he said and reached for his wallet.

The Hispanic clerk lifted his gaze to check out Evan's face. "Doing okay, buddy?"

"I will be. How much?"

The clerk checked the register and gave Evan the total as he bagged the bottles and snacks.

Not wanting to leave an electronic trace for anyone to follow, Evan counted off the bills and pushed it across. He accepted the change, receipt, and bag.

"Have a good trip, sir."

"Thanks," Evan mumbled, grabbing the coffee cup and left the station. Stepping outside in the heat, he searched again for any sign of the silver Porsche. Returning to the Jeep, he climbed in the driver's seat and glanced at the rear-view mirror.

Though he continued to check for the Porsche, he didn't expect George to wake up any time soon. The bastard had drank more than usual at the stuffy party he dragged Evan to and even more when they got home.

By the time George managed to open his eyes, Evan would be long gone, dust in the fucking wind.

Shoving fingers through his curly black hair, Evan grabbed a faded ball cap from his university and tugged it in place. He rubbed his hand over the scruffy morning beard he hadn't bothered to shave.

Time for him to get the hell out of Texas.

Turning on the engine, he hit the button to start the directions on his GPS unit, but turned down the volume. He shifted the gears into Drive and slammed his foot on the gas. The tires squealed and spit gravel out as he tore away from the station. He flicked a finger toward his past and George. Taking a turn, he made his way to the ramp leading to the highway.

Within minutes he drifted into place with the rest of the cars following the highway leading west through the northern Texas border with New Mexico. This stretch of blacktop highway would take him far away from Texas, away from the pain.

Reaching for the sunglasses, Evan pushed them up his nose. He squeezed the wheel with one hand as he pushed back the hurt and anger flooding him. Picking up the coffee cup, he blew through the tiny opening and took a tentative sip. It wasn't the best coffee, but it would keep him going for the next few miles. Setting it back in the holder, he connected his iPod to the Jeep and chose the mixed list of the country albums he'd added over the years.

The Rascal Flatts' song playing caused a smile to curl his lips as he listened to the lyrics. The girl in the song was doing the exact same thing he was doing: leaving a drunk bastard in the rear-view mirror as their wheels spun along the highway.

Several hours later, he crossed the Colorado border. His phone buzzed and rang as George hounded him with multiple calls. It got to the point where Evan couldn't stand the noise or harassment any longer. Following the exit, he left the highway and located a shopping center. He stormed into the nearest cell phone store, the phone continuing to buzz.

"I need a different phone with a new number, if possible."

"That one seems to be working fine," the clerk said.

"Doesn't matter, it has to be replaced. I only want some contacts transferred, not everything. Either I need a new cell or something else." Evan held up the phone. "I need to stop these damn calls. I'm being harassed by an ex."

The clerk blinked and took him through the options.

Evan chose the one he wanted and paid cash. He sighed when the clerk finally turned off the phone and popped the chip. He explained what he wanted transferred and nothing else onto a new chip. Grabbing a car charger and new case, he left the store. For the time being, he had thwarted George's attempts to contact him.

Moving down the sidewalk, he entered a larger store and went to the electronics area. He chose a cheap pay-as-you-go phone and paid in cash.

Hungry beyond the chocolate and snacks, he left the store and walked into the next shop. There he ordered two sandwiches and an extra-large iced tea. He also took the chance to empty his bladder. Washing his hands, he removed the ball cap to drag wet fingers through his hair and cupped the back of his neck. He sighed as the cool water hit his heated skin. Lifting his gaze, he stared at his image in the mirror. The morning shadow across his jaw gave him a scruffy look, which belied his haunted determined gaze.

Taking his bag from the clerk, he returned to the Jeep. First he plugged in the charger and connected it to the new phone. Breaking open the cheap phone's packaging, he followed directions to turn it on and located a decent signal. He dialed the number for his old home.

"Hello? Who the hell is this? What do you want?" George snarled into the phone.

"We're through, George," Evan said, his voice taut. "I'm done taking your shit. I'm long gone and you can't find me. I never want to talk to you again."

"You little prick! How could you leave me like this? No one leaves me. I'll hunt your fucking ass down. Wherever you go, no matter what you do, I can track you through licensing and AMA. Don't think I wouldn't."

"Try it. You don't know shit about using a computer. It's a fucking bluff, and I don't believe you. You'll never find me." Evan paused and used his final ace in the hole. "If you find me, I'll send everything about your physical and emotional abuse toward me and your alcohol use during rotations to the hospital and state medical board. Oh, did you forget, I'm an emergency doctor. I know damn well how to record and document every fucking thing you ever did to me. If you want to lose your reputation and position, try and find me. The moment I hear from you or see your face, the file will be sent."

Ending the call on George's stream of curses and threats, Evan turned it off, broke down the phone, and yanked out the chip.

As the phone charged, he drove to the gas station, turned everything off, and refilled the almost empty tank. Reaching inside, he pulled out the chips from his original phone and the cheap one. He stomped and pulverized them and the pay-as-you-go phone into the gravel and blacktop, not giving a damn about the odd looks. When everything was in enough tiny pieces, he picked them up and tossed them in the garbage. When the pump finished, he went inside and paid in cash.

Back in the Jeep once again, he returned to the highway, music playing and the new phone blessedly silent. Tugging out one of the sandwiches, cautious of his driving once he put it in cruise control, he devoured half of the sandwich. With his hunger satisfied, he checked the phone and dialed another number.

"Hello, this is Doctor Alfred Sampson. How can I help you?"

"Uncle Alfred, its Evan."

"Evan, my boy, it's good to hear from you. Are you safe? Did you get away?"

"Yes, I left him, Uncle."

"Good. It's good to hear from you, my boy. Is this a new number?"

"I had no choice. He blew up my phone with calls and texts. I pulverized the chip at the last stop."

"Did you call him?"

"From a cheap pay-as-you-go phone and destroyed it."

"He can't track your movements?"

"No. I'm using cash wherever I can."

"Good. Good. Where are you?"

"I'm driving through Colorado. I stopped in some place called Walsenburg for the phone, food, and gas. I'm back on Interstate-25 North and heading your way. I'll be there..." he paused and checked the GPS. "I have around another twenty hours, give or take depending on traffic."

"Don't drive all the way through. Stop and get some sleep when you need it. There are a few good places in Wyoming. I took the same route a couple of times."

"If I need it, I will, but I don't want to stop for long."

"Does he know where you're going?"

"No, I never mentioned your name or your country practice in Montana. He wouldn't even dream of stepping anywhere outside of a city street. Only my best friend knows, and he never crosses path with George."

"Can you trust your friend?"

"He helped me with the plans to leave."

"I look forward to seeing you. I could use your help around this place. I started the paperwork to let you practice medicine up here with a lawyer friend, who I told the situation to help hide you from George."

"I'm grateful you're giving me a new start. Can you trust him?"

"I've known him longer than you've been alive, boy."

"Who is it?"

"His name is J. Parker Wallace of the Walker, Wallace & Partners firm. It's located in Whitepine."

"Whitepine? I thought I'm heading to Kalispell?"

"The clinic is in between them. There's a small cabin attached to the clinic where you can live until you find something more permanent."

"Thanks, Uncle Alfred. I don't know what I would have done."

"You're a resourceful young man. You would have found a way to leave him."

"The sight of your email and offer took a huge weight off me. Along with my friend's urging, it gave me the push I needed."

"Happy to hear I could help some little bit. Drive safe. Don't push yourself. You'll get here when you can. There's no rush now that you're outta Texas, son."

"Thanks again, Uncle."

"See you soon," Alfred said and hung up.

Placing the phone back to let it continue to charge, Evan turned up the music.

As the miles and hours ticked away, he passed signs for Pueblo, Colorado Springs, and Denver. After Denver he took a ramp to refill the tank, hit the restroom, and purchase coffee. Before climbing back in, he stretched and moved his achy limbs. Gaining a little more energy, he returned to the highway, merging back onto I-25 North with the mess of other cars, trucks, and regular folks going about their normal day.

His day had been anything but normal.

Another four hours later, he crossed well into Wyoming. As it got darker, he located the first major city and followed a ramp with a sign noting multiple motels. He chose the Motel 6 and followed directions until he saw the sign. Turning into the parking lot by the main entrance, he parked and left with his new phone and wallet. Heading to reception, he waited a moment to speak with a clerk.

"Hello and welcome to Motel 6. Do you have a reservation?" the young woman said with a smile.

"No, but I'm hoping to get a single room for the night."

"Sure, we have some available." She typed things into the system and offered options.

"Non-smoking and king-size."

"We don't have any king beds. I can give you a single queen bed."

"Fine."

"I'll need a bit of information and a government-issued ID."

Evan slid out the Texas driver's license and handed it over.

"Wow. You're a long way from home."

"Road trip."

"Those are fun," she said and entered the information. "Would you like to pay with a credit card?"

"Cash. I can pay for the room now."

"Check-out is before noon tomorrow."

"I'll be leaving earlier."

She finished the check-in process and gave him the amount.

Evan counted out the cash and placed it on the counter. She checked his count, placed it in the register, and printed out the receipt. He took the papers and his ID back. He watched her set up a room card and slid it in a small envelope. She wrote a number on the front and explained where the room was and to park.

"Thanks, appreciate it."

"You're welcome. Have a good night, and enjoy your stay at Motel 6. If there is any trouble, don't hesitate to contact the desk."

Evan went to the glass doors, opened one for a talkative family returning from dinner. He headed to the Jeep and drove around to the far side. Parking again, he picked up the last sandwich, a bottle of water, and his overnight bag. With a click of the locks, he climbed the stairs to the second floor and located the room. He shoved the card in the reader and stepped inside to the decent size room. He checked over the single queen bed, tiny kitchenette, bathroom, and a desk area. Hanging the *Do Not Disturb* sign, he locked and flipped the lever in place. He placed the food and water in the tiny fridge, adjusted the thermostat to remove some of the stuffiness, and dropped the bag on the bed. He sat down hard on the edge.

Picking up the phone, he dialed his uncle's number.

"This is Doctor Alfred Sampson, how can I help you?"

"Hey, it's me."

"Need to figure out how to save this number in my contacts. Darn it," his uncle grumped and asked, "Where are you, son?"

"I stopped for the night in Casper at a motel."

"Good. Get some rest."

"I'll do my best."

"You're safe, son. You're away from him and Texas."

"I still believe he's somehow following me."

"That's the lingering fear and guilt inside you. As you said, you covered your tracks. He doesn't know. Do you have your laptop?"

"Yes, he never knew any passwords or log-ons. I changed them every few weeks and again a couple of days before I left. He knows the bare basics of computers and is constantly losing his passwords. Though he threatened to call or track me through the state boards, he has no idea how to do it. Plus, I warned him if he did track me down, I would ruin everything in his life."

"You documented everything, didn't you?" his uncle said.

"It's what any good ER doctor would do when confronted with an abused patient."

"Good for you, son."

"At least I did something right."

"You did more than one thing right. He doesn't know your plans. Your friend will say he knows nothing and feels betrayed at your leaving. Even if he's bold enough to try anything, he can't report your car missing because you're alone on the registration. You're too old and capable for him to put out a missing person's report. You're safe, my boy."

"Thanks for the reminder."

"I think you'll need a couple of them until you feel safe. Get some sleep. See you tomorrow," Alfred said.

"Night, Uncle."

Ending the call again, Evan kicked off his shoes and opened the bag. As a doctor and knowing more than he should about germs, he yanked out a pack of sanitizer cleansing wipes and used them on all the hard surfaces. Feeling a little better, he shoved the pack back in his bag. Pulling out his toiletries kit, he went to the bathroom. He set out the supplies, turned on the shower, and returned to the main room. Locating the remote, he turned on the television and put it on some random news channel. Tugging off the rest of his clothes until just the boxers remained, he tossed them on the bed.

Returning to the shower, he dropped the boxers, grabbed his personal, multi-use cleanser, and stepped inside the shower. Lifting his head back, he let the somewhat warm water pound down upon his tense frame.

Finishing, he dried off, wrapping the towel around his waist. Standing in front of the mirror, he scratched at the thicker growth along his jaw. Picking up his electric razor, he stood over the sink and removed the wiry strands that would annoy him as he slept.

Finishing the late shave, he cleaned the mess and completed his evening routine with some moisturizing lotion. He knew he was good-looking and wanted to keep up his appearance, even in the middle of the country. Grabbing another thin motel towel, he scrubbed his hair dry

Leaning closer, Evan gasped as he feathered the hair above his ears. "Sonofa... Damn stress gave me gray hairs. Shit. So not fair."

Shaking it off, he returned to the room. Digging out a pair of sleep pants, he loosened the towel and stepped into them. He added a pair of soft socks. Tossing the towels into the bathroom, he pulled out the bottle and sandwich. Sitting cross-legged on the bed, he devoured the sandwich and clicked over to a national channel to check out the latest news. There was nothing on the news about a missing doctor from Texas, not even a blip.

Cursing when he realized he forgot to call the hospital, Evan picked up the phone. He dialed the number for his friend and the Chief of Emergency Medicine, Carson Reed. When he tried to explain it was due to personal reasons, Carson demanded more of an answer. As the Senior ER Attending physician, Evan realized Carson didn't want to lose him to a bogus reason. No senior physician would up and quit for no damn reason. Finally, Evan told Carson about being in an abusive relationship and he needed to change everything, including his career and location. He didn't go into depth, but made sure to get the urgency of the situation through to Carson. When Carson accepted his request, Evan added he didn't expect severance since he quit. He also didn't want George to track the check or paperwork. With several apologies, he ended the call with a sick stomach about abandoning the ER. He thought about the wonderful nurses, residents and interns along with the non-medical staff who became friends. Even though he didn't get a chance to say good-bye to, it was for the best. The less they knew, the less they could pass on anything.

There was one other doctor he could trust with all the details. Turning the phone a couple of times in his hands, he dialed another number.

"Umm. Yeah." A loud yawn escaped over the phone. "Sorry. Hello?" a sleepy voice asked.

"Lucas?"

"Evan? Is that you?"

"Yes, it's me."

The voice became clearer in almost a second. "Are you safe?"

Closing his eyes at the voice of his best friend, the one who helped him plan the escape from the destruction of his life, Evan let out a sigh. "Yes, I'm safe. I'm out of Texas."

"Thank fucking God. Can he track you?"

"No, I got rid of my phone and picked up a new one with a different number. Sorry, I didn't check the time. Did I wake you?"

"Late emergency surgery. Screw sleep. When did you get out of town?"

"Before sunrise. He was drunk from the party and passed out. Took the chance. I packed my stuff and drove away."

"Where are you?"

"Holding up in a motel in Wyoming."

"Heading north?"

"Yes, only you know."

"You know I wouldn't tell anyone where you are."

"I know. I never mentioned anyone up here to George or others in the ER to keep it a safe option. Other than you, I didn't trust anyone else due to George's reputation and status."

"Shit, Jesus, man, I didn't know it was that bad. What about the hospital?"

"I called and said I quit due to personal reasons. My life in Texas is done, except for our friendship."

"When you asked me to help you get away, I didn't think things had gone as far as they did. Shit, this is all messed up." Lucas sighed over the phone. "We'll talk again. Call when you settle in. Just so I know you're all right."

"Will do. Go back to sleep, Lucas, sorry I woke you."

"Talking to you was more important. If I could, I would strangle the bastard along with a bunch of other fellas. We'll make sure the Board knows what he's doing. I'm sure you can't be the first partner he abused..."

"I'm sure he has more traumatized victims in his closet, but they're too afraid to say anything against him, especially if they're also in the hospital community." Evan dragged fingers through his damp hair and wished he could help George's other victims. "Don't put yourself on his radar, or he'll turn his anger against you."

"I know. I'll keep an eye on things and see what he tries. If I learn he finds you, we'll release the file and ruin his life. You trusted me with a copy of your report for a reason, I'll make sure to use it when necessary. I have your back, E. Always."

"Love ya, man."

"Same here, E. Take care."

"Bye, Lucas." Evan hung up the call and dropped backwards on the bed.

He never thought separating himself from the rest of his life would be so difficult. He would miss the crazy times with his best friend, even at odd moments within the hospital.

Chapter Two

Absently rubbing and massaging his left wrist, Joshua Holmwood watched the mountains tower over them while the Midnight Twang tour bus brought them home from the latest series of gigs up and down the west coast. They had traveled from Southern California through to Canada for the last four months. All of them were road-weary and ready for the quiet life upon the Montana ranch.

The twinge and ache in his wrist told him there were problems. It ached worse after playing the violin for hours during their concerts and practicing for more, but this was his life.

Since Kaden joined the band, they only got better with every practice. Interest in Midnight Twang was at an all-time high. Their songs were high on the all the streaming Country lists with thousands of downloads. There were rumors circulating about a contract with a Nashville record label.

Josh couldn't let down the band, not when all their hard work was finally paying off. They were so close to the big-time.

Working his way to the front of the bus, Josh watched Kaden bend over to speak with their driver. A retired long-haul truck driver, Ernie joined them on the road, joking how his wife was ready to kick him out if he didn't do something soon. Once he entered the bus, he said he was in pure heaven the minute he sat in the chair and stared at the controls.

After speaking, Kaden paused at the galley for a bag of snacks and a couple of drinks. Once Josh saw the bright bag of Crunchy Cheetos, he knew Sage, his partner, craved them. Sage was the only one to eat an entire bag on his own when he scribbled new lyrics.

Kaden paused next to Josh's bench. "Hey, Josh, come on back and talk with us." Kaden nodded toward the back of the bus he shared with Sage. As the designated leaders of the band and partners, no one argued about the living arrangements.

"Yeah, sure," Josh said as he left his quiet bench seat and followed Kaden to the back area.

Though they weren't with a record company or making large amounts of money, Kaden refused to travel in the broken down, extended camper and van they used on earlier road trips. Before this trip, he had a bus completely decked out with this back area, sleeping areas for the others, a kitchen/general area, and a comfortable front driver's deck. When they stopped for the night, sections of the bus expanded out to give them additional sleeping and moving around room. Ernie's chair stretched out and turned into a comfortable bunk, and he didn't let anyone else come near it.

Closed off with a couple of curtains and walls for a private area for the couple, Josh grinned at finding they'd converted the bed back into a bench and table.

Kaden nudged his belly with an elbow. "What? Think I'll take you back after a bit of sexy time? Please. Now that I have him back in my life, I don't share," he teased.

Josh laughed hard.

Stepping past the curtain, they found Sage sitting at the table, music sheets and a notebook spread out. An acoustic guitar rested next to him. Sage tapped a pencil in a rhythmic pattern on the table, humming under his breath, as he erased and altered something on the notebook.

"Hey, hon, recharge your batteries. Got Josh here," Kaden said as he dropped the bag of Cheetos and a stack of napkins. He cracked the bottle of flavored water and set it by Sage's hand.

Still lost in lyrics, Sage didn't acknowledge either one of them.

Kaden plopped hard next to Sage, deliberately using his weight to make the cushion rock. He pointed Josh to the other bench. Shifting around for a few sections, he uncovered a remote and lowered the flat panel television back into its hideaway spot. He cracked open a bottle of soda and drank half of it. He glanced from their munchies to Josh and blushed. "Sorry, stupid me. Did you want something?"

"Had something earlier. What do you need from me?" Josh asked, glancing at Sage and back to Kaden.

"He's listening, just not giving us his full attention," Kaden said with a smile. He nudged Sage's side with his elbow. "How are you doing? Are you feeling okay?"

Josh blinked in surprise at the query. "I'm good."

"You dropped and covered several notes during the last concert. You changed a couple others," Sage said, lifting his gaze to find Josh. "It didn't sound bad, just unexpected."

Josh stared at the wood-grained tabletop and traced one line with his finger.

"What's going on with your hands?" Kaden asked. "I see you massaging it after practice and holding your left hand close to your chest as if protecting it after concerts. You're popping lots of ibuprofen, using ice packs, and heating pads."

"Thought I was hiding it better."

"Nope. Not from us, buddy. What's happening? We can't help if you don't tell us," Kaden said.

"I don't want to disappoint either of you or leave the band."

"Why would you?"

"My entire left hand is giving me some trouble. The last two fingers are numb, and, at times during practices and concerts, I can't feel the strings. My wrist aches while supporting the violin and collapses in adding to the strain," Josh said.

"Lay your forearms across the table," Sage said.

With a sigh, Josh placed his wrist, palm up, on the table. He rested his right wrist nearby for comparison.

"It's swollen, and these fingers do feel a little colder than the others," Sage said, touching the area with gentle fingers. "What else are you feeling?"

"I get a tingling numbing sensation from my elbow down to my fourth and fifth fingers on my left hand. I saw a doctor before the tour."

"Doc Sampson?"

"No, he wasn't there. It was someone else. He said it was tendonitis and to rest it. If I had trouble, take the ibuprofen, perform some stretches and warm-ups, and use a brace for evenings when I sleep. It isn't getting better," Josh said. His voice thickened at the simple scary thought of not being able to play his violin.

"Do you have the brace with you?"

"Yeah, I stash it in my cubby."

"Okay. We already planned for the entire band to enjoy some downtime when we get home. We'll concentrate on the ranch and everyday stuff. We can jam and practice if they want, but nothing mandatory. If we want to work on the new songs, we can, but I still need to pull together everything," Sage said and glanced at Kaden. "We all need a break, not just you."

"I agree. We all need a break and back to normal daily living to recharge," Kaden said.

"During this time, I want you to rest completely, Josh. Oh wait, are you going back to your parents' place for a few weeks?"

"That was the plan, but I could change it."

"Whatever is best for you, but you know there's plenty of room for you to stay here. Either way, make sure you keep up with the therapies and brace. We'll change your chores around the ranch, so you don't have rely on your wrist as much. You can work more in the training circle." Sage held up a hand to stop Josh's protest. "We have enough help to cover you. Charlie hired a couple more hands while we were gone. The new bunkhouse is finished, so everyone won't be so cramped in the old one."

"Also, we'll get Doc Sampson to come by and check you over. We'll ask if there are alternatives and other doctors who can help. No matter where you need to go or what has to be done, we'll cover you," Kaden said. "Either under the ranch or the band, we have insurance to protect everyone. Time to use it to help you get the medical support."

"What if we get the contract and have to perform?" Josh asked. "I don't want to let you guys down or the rest of the band."

"It's still rumors and talk, nothing is firm. If we get lucky and things come through, we'll figure it out. You're our brother, and we want you healthy."

Josh lifted his good hand and shoved fingers through his hair, messing up the layers.

Stretching across the table, Kaden laid his hand on Josh's shoulder. "Hey. We'll get you through this. Okay?"

Unable to say anything, Josh nodded multiple times as his mind raced with thoughts. He prayed he wouldn't lose his ability to play.

Chapter Three

After another eight hours on the road, Evan made it to the Flathead County Clinic between Kalispell and Whitepine, Montana. His uncle had created this place to get a more centralized location and the ability to run house calls to the different smaller towns and ranches throughout the county. As his uncle promised, Evan located the A-frame log cabin tucked behind the clinic.

Emptying out the Jeep, Evan crashed onto the lavender-scented sheets and slept for another six hours. He didn't sleep much at the motel, waking at every sound, fearful it was George, hot on his trail.

Waking to the smell of tomatoes, basil, and garlic, Evan rolled out bed, dragging both hands through his hair and scratched at the scraggly beard. He stumbled down from the loft and saw his uncle in the kitchen. A couple of big pots were on the burners.

"Is that your infamous basil tomato sauce?" Evan asked as an introduction.

Alfred Sampson turned with a big smile curling his lips. He licked sauce off his thumb and wiped his hands on a towel. Opening his arms, he walked across the floor and wrapped Evan in a huge bear hug. Taller and broader than Evan, he always did resemble a big bear to him since he was a kid. Even with the graying hair and wrinkles earned by hours in the sun and hard work, Alfred remained a huge presence.

Sinking against his uncle's strong frame, Evan tightened his arms around Alfred and pressed his face against the broad shoulder. To his horror, sobs wracked his worn, exhausted body and mind. He cracked and let it out as his uncle soothed him. By the time he finished, he felt drained of everything inside him.

"Didn't mean to fall apart on you," Evan said.

"You've been wound up tight for a while. Doing better?"

"Yes, a little better. Damn bastard for causing all this shit." Evan stepped back and rubbed his hands against his eyes. He knew they were probably swollen and red along with a runny nose. He wasn't a pretty crier when he let it out. With a quick search, he found a box of tissues and yanked out a couple to clean himself.

"I'm sure it'll hit you at odd times."

"What will hit? The anger and pain? Yes, the emotions flare up every once in a while."

"Do you need something to ease the way?"

"No, I don't want any medication. I don't want to go down that path and rely on them."

"If you change your mind, I'll help you."

"Thanks, Uncle, but I want to fight through this on my own. If the depression lasts, I'll let you know."

"How about I put some good food in your belly?"

"Food always helps, right?"

Alfred shrugged. "Things look better with a full belly. It's what your grandma always told us boys while she cooked up a pot of her sauce."

"This is her recipe?"

"Yup. Didn't your dad teach you?"

Evan shook his head. "No, he was always working."

"Sorry to say, but it's why he's in the ground now with your mama. Never took a moment to step back and breathe, and his heart gave up on him. I hope you don't follow his lead," Alfred said, waving a hand at his nephew.

"The hospital kept me going and filled with all kinds of business, especially after they put me in charge of the residents. Didn't have much downtime, even at home since George was the party addict. I'll learn to chill out better while staying here with you. You're still a spry, happy go-lucky fellow."

"Don'tcha know it. All the local widows still hit on me whenever they get a chance. I'm a lucky fella." Alfred let out a belly laugh as he returned to the kitchen. He dished up piles of spaghetti and homemade sauce. He lowered the plates on the table he set earlier.

Following his uncle, Evan dropped in the opposite chair and enjoyed the delicious meal. Halfway through he leaned back, sipping at the fresh iced tea. "Tell me about the clinic and house calls."

"You don't want to wait and settle in."

"No, I'll only commiserate and wallow. I need to keep busy," Evan said with another sip. "How did you start all of this? Not many doctors make house calls, unless you're a large animal vet, and it's fairly mandatory."

"Around here I felt it was rather necessary. Most folks are farmers or ranchers. They're salt-of-the-earth type folks who work from sun-up to sun-down to care for their land and animals. As you said, a large animal vet goes to them, so why not a human doc? I have hours for the clinic and others for when I can drive around the county."

"Has it only been you doing all this?"

"No, as I got older, I brought on another pair of doctors, more nurses, and two nurse practitioners. We all have different backgrounds and specialties to help everyone within the community. Still, there's always room for a brilliant young doctor who happens to also be my favorite nephew," Alfred said, lifting his gaze with a grin.

"Hopefully, I'm worthy of the praise."

"While you may have had rotten taste in men, you're a brilliant doctor." Alfred wagged a finger toward him. "Never forget that."

"You're pretty darn good at giving pep-talks."

"I have a lot of years and experience to pull from, my boy." Evan laughed. "That's the smiling boy I knew was hiding in there."

Evan continued to laugh until he held his belly as it ached. When it calmed down, he waved a hand. "Really. Tell me about the clinic and your patients."

Chuckling back as they continued dinner, Alfred explained how the concept of a mobile clinic worked. While he talked, he rose and went toward the front entrance. Reaching into the large bag he left earlier, he pulled out an expandable folder and returned to the table. He opened the folder and tugged out multiple folders with different names.

"What's this?"

"Your upcoming appointments."

"My what?"

"Even though I wanted you to take some time, I knew you wouldn't. Since you confirmed coming, I pulled together some files to help you to jump right into things and get out in the field. As you said, it'll help you get your mind off things."

"I have no supplies or any idea where I'm going."

"Every morning or evening, depending on their shifts, everyone restocks their supplies from the clinic supply room. I'll help you build your initial bag and stock. In the morning we'll load up your Jeep. I'll add a couple of maps to go along with your GPS system."

"They have no idea who I am."

"While you're getting used to the patients and them to you, I figure you can wear your white coat."

"While on house calls?"

"Best way to tell them right away about who you are. You can take it off during the visit when everyone is comfortable."

"Sounds like a decent idea."

"It's only for the first few weeks. Once you accepted my offer, I've been passing around word of your arrival, and I have car magnets."

"Car magnets?"

"They're signs of the clinic's logo. I had them made for everyone's vehicle. It's amazing what you can find these days online. You'll have a magnet for the driver's side door and on the back."

Evan chuckled at his uncle's interest in simple magnets. "You trust me to jump in with both feet and not fall apart."

"You're a damn good doctor. If you need a break, disappear somewhere, and take the time."

"Why can't I handle the clinic's patients for a few days to get comfortable?"

"You'll handle a couple of early appointments to get used to things. By eleven, you'll get on the road and start taking care of the others. Here's an appointment calendar and a notebook to keep all your notes, travel times, and other information."

Flipping the pages of the appointment book, Evan glanced at his uncle. "Can I bring this into the twenty-first century and do everything on my tablet?"

Alfred let out another big belly laugh. "Do whatever you want with it, son. Just follow the calendar, get to as many folks as you can, but give everyone the time and care they need and personal attention."

"As you would do for any patient," Evan said.

"Smart ass." Alfred shook his head with a big smile. "Either way, make sure you turn in everything at the end of each week for updates to all files, insurance and accounting programs."

"Will do." Evan flipped through the folders. "Is this the background history for each patient?"

"Yes, this one I'm quite worried about, considering her condition. This is a lovely lady named Carolyn Wallstatt. She lives at the Triple W Ranch and Stables," Alfred said as he tugged out a particular folder. "She's suffering from Alzheimer's and believes it's more than thirty years in the past. One day, she left the main house for a walk and went to the original cabin built by her husband's grandfather. She never left."

"Poor lady. What about her family?"

"Her husband died from an unexpected heart attack. I didn't even predict it because he was as healthy as one of his horses. Something happened to put his rhythm off track, and he couldn't recover. His death hit her hard.

"They have three children together, two sons and a daughter. Carolyn's sister, Patricia, lives with her and is one of the few who can speak with Carolyn and knows about those early years. She doesn't recognize her grown children. In her mind, Carolyn believes she's a newlywed and starting a brand-new life with her husband. Her husband is working on the ranch and adding onto the main house," Alfred explained.

"Wow. She's in the later stages of the illness."

"Yes."

"What type of therapies have you tried?"

"I've tried different medications and therapies, but nothing seems to help her. She's one of those patients that don't respond to medication." Alfred tapped his fingers on the folder. "For another opinion and ideas, I want you to meet her and see what you think of the situation. The family refuses to put her in hospice or full-time care since it would upset her further."

"Will my visit upset her?"

"I think she'll believe you're a younger me when I started my practice after medical school."

"A younger you, huh?"

"Well... We do have the same coloring."

"Sampson coloring."

Alfred chuckled and nodded. "Blood runs true in our family."

"Do you want me to go to the Triple W first?"

"Please, Patricia mentioned her lucid moments are lessening along with her speech and movements. She said Carolyn's coloring is off and something else is happening. From my last visit, I think she developed a form of cancer."

"Cancer?"

"Possibly pancreas or liver, but without tests I'm not sure. If we brought her to the clinic or hospital..."

"It would be bad."

"Shock to her and her system. Patricia and Carolyn's younger son don't want to prolong her pain and life. They want to support her as long as possible but don't want to extend things with unnecessary treatments."

"She could be closer to the end, if she has an advanced cancer."

"It's what I believe. Call me once you speak with her and we can discuss options."

"If she doesn't leave, I don't know how much more we could do." Evan shrugged. "We'll have to see about bringing hospice care to her."

"It wouldn't be the first time I helped a family support a patient at home."

"What about the others?"

Alfred took him through the rest of the folders and what Evan could expect.

Chapter Four

Listening to the local radio station playing country rock music, Evan tapped his fingers on the steering wheel and mouthed the lyrics. His love of country music grew while he enjoyed watching the hilarious and intriguing bromance on *The Voice* between the tattooed rocker and soulful country cowboy. Every time the show came on, he couldn't wait to watch the next banter between them. He kept the beat of country star's latest song playing.

While working in the clinic that morning, Evan realized the difference between large cities and small towns. He learned to take his time with each patient, listening to all the gossip and the endless questions. He enjoyed everyone's friendly nature and acceptance of his presence. That afternoon, he became good friends with his GPS system and detailed maps while driving through the crazy country roads.

As he promised his uncle, he headed straight for his first appointment. He traveled toward the mountains and Glacier National Park, to the small town called Whitepine. According to the GPS, the ranch was a little over twenty miles from the clinic. Unlike the plains and finicky weather of Texas, he found himself surrounded by vast ranches and rolling hills of grass and thick forests and a skyline filled with mountains.

Reaching the outskirts of Whitepine, he needed to locate a ranch called Triple W. From their conversation the night before, his uncle explained the Wallstatt family had owned the land for several generations, and now the youngest generation ran the stables. Though, out of the three children, only the younger son remained on the land, working it with a trusted foreman. The older son was in the military.

The daughter married a police officer and moved south to Missoula with him.

Spotting a sign, Evan slowed the Jeep.

"Ahh, there you are," he said and turned onto the dirt road. He enjoyed the excellent shock system as the tires dipped and hit the nasty potholes. "Yeah. This is fun." A little further down, he checked out the iron and wood sign arching over the wood with iron gates opened to visitors. Looking at both gates, he realized a portion created a 'W' in the middle when closed.

On either side of the road to the main house—if you could call it a road—he checked out the expansive grasslands fenced in along with arenas where horses pranced or stood. He didn't know much about horses, but he noticed these were sleek and gorgeous, full of colors from the golden sun to the deepest red.

A cowboy stepped out of the closest barn and waved his hat. He pointed and led him toward an open area. Figuring this meant him, Evan followed directions and stopped by other dusty and battered trucks. He turned off the engine and stepped out onto the ground, luckily not in a stinky pile. The cowboy boots he purchased long ago in a Texas shop fit in around here.

"Hello there, sorry about that, but the bus is on its way and will need room to park," the cowboy said, a definite county twang filling his words. Montana accents were far different from the Texan drawl or twang.

"Bus?"

"Hmm. Some of the boys created a country-rock group, doing quite well, and they just finished a tour up and down the west coast. They're scheduled to come back within the next few hours." The cowboy put his Stetson back in place and tugged on the brim. "How can I help you? Do you work with the clinic?"

Evan removed his sunglasses and hooked them from his opened-neck, button-down shirt. "In a way, yes, I'm the newest doctor for the clinic. I'm Doctor Evan Sampson. I'm Doctor Alfred Sampson's nephew. He asked me to be the new traveling doctor for this section of the county." As his uncle suggested, he picked up his white doctor's coat and tugged it over his shirt and pants. "Sorry, my uncle suggested I wear the coat for the first few visits."

"Welcome to the Triple W, Doc. I'm the foreman, Charlie Wyght. Good suggestion on it. Gives us a heads up about who you are, if we didn't notice those crazy magnets."

Evan chuckled as he glanced back to see the magnet attached to the door. "My uncle's latest Internet find." He cleared his throat and looked back at Charlie. "Are you one of the Ws?"

"Pardon… Oh, in the name. Nope. The original founders were the three Wallstatt brothers. The current generation is from the oldest brother." Adjusting the Stetson, Charlie changed the subject for them and asked, "Whatcha here for, Doc?"

"I'm here for an appointment with Carolyn Wallstatt."

"I'm guessing Miz Patti called it in and didn't alert me. I apologize."

"Not a problem. Is Miss Carolyn in the house?"

"No, sir, she went for a walk one afternoon and ended up at the old cabin. She never left."

"Right. Yes. I'm sorry, my uncle mentioned something about that before." Evan rubbed his temples, wondering what was happening with his memory.

"I'm betting you had a lot of information thrown at you since you arrived…"

"Yesterday. I arrived yesterday."

"From Texas?"

"Yes."

"Thought I picked up the twang. Welcome to Montana, Doc."

"Thank you. It's quite different up here."

"The mountains and national forest give things quite a different appearance."

"Yes, they do, a beauty in their own right."

"If you can get your bag, I'll take you to the old cabin on our four-by-four."

"Thank you," Evan said. He returned to the Jeep, pulled out the large bag and backpack from the back. He locked it up and followed the older cowboy. He slid the sunglasses back onto his face to shade his eyes from the bright Montana sun.

"Climb on in," Charlie said as he slid in the driver's seat and started the off-road vehicle.

Reaching the small cabin within a few minutes, Evan stepped out, slid his backpack over one shoulder and grabbed the bag. He pulled off the glasses and slid them in a pocket. He dragged his fingers through his hair, smoothing it after the brief ride and walked up to the porch. He knocked on the door.

The door opened to reveal a lady with silver hair pulled in a loose bun and a soft blue dress. She adjusted the glasses on her nose. "Hello."

"Hello, I'm Doctor Evan Sampson. Doctor Alfred, my uncle, asked me to check on Carolyn Wallstatt. Are you her sister, Patricia Carter?"

"I am and thank you for coming. I'm worried about her. Call me Patti, please," Patti said, stepping back to let Evan in the home. She waved her hand toward the opposite corner.

Turning, Evan saw a tiny lady curled in a rocking chair by the fireplace. A crocheted blanket wrapped around her shoulders while another covered her lap. Glasses perched on her nose, but she stared at the fireplace.

"Carrie, hon, look who's here," Patti said as she moved to touch her sister's shoulder.

It took a few moments, but the lady twisted to look at her sister and beyond. Though there wasn't much within her gaze, her eyes remained a brilliant green. Her lips curled with a shaky smile. "Doctor Sampson, I see you did well on your exams and made your mama proud. Look at you in your white coat."

Pausing at the soft words, Evan realized Carolyn thought he was his uncle. He smiled and crouched next to the chair. He placed both bags on the floor. "I passed them, Mrs. Wallstatt, and she is proud."

Carolyn patted his hand. "You're a good boy. Say hello to your mama for me."

"I will, ma'am. How are you doing today?"

She grabbed a laced-edge handkerchief and raised it to her lips. She coughed hard, rattling her entire body. "I'm afraid I don't feel well."

"How about letting me take a quick look? We'll see if we can get you to feeling a bit better." Evan opened the bag and started his examination. At the sight of the slightly jaundiced skin, he knew his uncle's hunch about cancer would turn up correct. If it was, he figured things wouldn't end well.

A half hour later, Evan carried the bags to his Jeep. He pulled out his tablet, where he transferred all the files Alfred gave him the previous night and created his own calendar and travel log. He brought up the records for Carolyn and picked up his cell phone.

"Excuse me, Doc, but what do you think?" Charlie shuffled from one foot to the other.

Evan checked some of the notes his uncle made from a previous visit and answered Charlie. "It's not good news. She's in the last stages of the cancer my uncle suspected. I can't confirm if it's liver or pancreatic, but either way, it isn't good. Without treatment or support, it'll be painful for her. Where are her children?"

"Her oldest son is a Marine. The bus is due back with her younger son, Sage—" Charlie paused as several loud horns blared and the rumble of a large diesel engine rolled toward them. "There it is. Can you wait?"

"For this case, yes, I'll wait and speak with them now. Her treatment can't wait." Evan watched the decorated, tricked-out bus move around the circular driveway and park back toward the driveway. The door slid back, and a large group of folks stepped down the stairs, laughing and joking with one another. Most of them held backpacks, duffel bags, and instrument cases.

Two young men were last to leave. Though one followed the other, they kept their hands clasped together. It was an obvious display of affection. One wore a faded ball cap while the other sported a battered, fedora type of hat. They each carried a large duffel bag on their shoulders.

Evan was surprised to find a gay couple out and proud up here.

"Sage, Kaden, come over here," Charlie called, waving his hat to get their attention.

The couple changed direction toward Charlie. The rest of the group followed, hanging back a few steps.

The one with the faded ball cap dropped his bag and hugged Charlie. "Hey, how is everything going?"

"Hey there, Charlie," the other young man in the fedora said as he picked up the other man's bag.

After the hug, Charlie waved a hand around the group. "Sage Wallstatt and Kaden Carmody, this is Doctor Evan Sampson. He's Doc Alfred's nephew and new partner at the clinic. He came to look over your mama, Sage."

Sage looked from Kaden, to Charlie, and then Evan. "What about Mama? Is her condition deteriorating?"

"It isn't good, son," Charlie said. "There is more than her Alzheimer's."

"What is wrong with Mama? Why didn't you call me sooner about this?" Taller than Evan, Sage lowered his gaze to reveal a darker hazel-green color than his mother's pure green.

"We weren't sure what was happening with her, and Miz Patti didn't want your tour disturbed."

Evan hated this part of being a doctor, of giving bad news to the family. "Hello, Mr. Wallstatt, I'm sorry to give you the news like this. As my uncle suspected, and I concur with the diagnosis, your mother's cancer is in the final stages. I'm so sorry."

Sage's body became limp at the news. Dropping the bags, Kaden managed to hold him on his feet thanks to quick reflexes. Kaden took a step back to take Sage's sudden weight but steadied both of them. The rest of the group gathered in a show of support and solidarity.

Evan watched one of the men move closer. He noticed a protective brace around the left wrist and hand. His doctor's interest became peaked. When he lifted his gaze to find deep green eyes surrounded by lush lashes and caramel-gold hair under the Stetson, the rest of him became interested. His body stirred with arousal, so surprising after the hell he went through with George. Still, the way the lean cowboy's body filled the faded denim and decorated T-shirt was just how he enjoyed a lover.

The tall cowboy seemed to have felt Evan's gaze upon him and moved to meet his gaze. A corner of his mouth tilted in a grin as he winked. He didn't do more, not in the presence of his hurt friend.

Clearing his throat and adjusting his stance, Evan pushed back the lusty feelings to concentrate on the reason he stood there. While he was lost in checking out the cowboy, Kaden continued to soothe his boyfriend.

"Sage, easy, breathe, hon, breathe. Stay with me," Kaden said, keeping his voice low and soothing. He pressed soft kisses to Sage's temple, nudging the cap back with his nose. He rubbed circles with his hand across Sage's back.

Swallowing hard, his jaw working, Sage curled against Kaden. His ball cap shifting askew as he pressed closer. "How long?" Sage managed to ask after Kaden calmed him down. He lifted his gaze to find Evan. The pain-filled look within the hazel-green eyes shattered.

His stomach clenched at the shattered look. Evan hated giving him more news. "I'm not sure. It's different with every patient, and she's one stubborn, determined lady. Without proper diagnosis and tests to confirm the type and extent of cancer, I can't give a firm answer."

"That's my mama. What do you recommend?"

"Usually, at this stage, my first recommendation would be that she needs to go to hospice. Without care and medical support, she'll be in pain," Evan said.

"She won't leave the cabin. She hasn't since she walked away one afternoon," Sage said.

"Can we bring the support to her? I can cover the expense," Kaden said.

"My uncle mentioned the same thing when we spoke about her case. I believe we can create a home care system." Evan dragged fingers through his hair and let out a sigh. "I need to speak with my uncle. I'm sure he knows of a local hospice that can send the equipment we need along with a trained nurse."

"Aunt Patti will help convince her to accept the help. She's good with Mama," Sage said, wiping his hand against his face.

Wanting to hear confirmation about the situation from Sage, Evan asked, "What about you?"

"Mama lives in a time before she had any babies with Daddy. They're newlyweds and moved to the cabin while Daddy builds upon the larger main house." Curling back against Kaden, Sage shook her head. "I upset the balance if I say hello. My brother used to resemble our father better, but I haven't spoken to him in some time. He's in the military."

Evan stared down at the ground. The situation was indeed delicate and would need care in how he handled things.

"What can we do?" Charlie asked.

"Perhaps we should all go inside, get something to drink, and get comfortable. This will take more than a talk out here," one of the other young men said.

Realizing the new speaker was the tall cowboy he eyed earlier, Evan licked his lower lip as if his mouth was suddenly dry. The whiskey-smooth voice sounded like velvet along his senses and went so well with the rest of him. Evan felt his body respond again to the man. He checked out the cowboy a little closer, this time noticing the pair of violin cases dangled from his free hand.

The cowboy met Evan's glance, did his own check-over from Evan's boots, along the white coat, and up to his hair. He tilted his head with another laconic grin.

Did he know what Evan felt at that moment?

"You're right, Josh. We're sorry, Doctor, excuse our lack of hospitality. It's a little hot out here," Kaden said with a shrug.

"I heard all of you came off a long road trip. I didn't expect anything more than a visit with Miss Carolyn and your aunt."

"Would you please follow us inside, Doctor?" Kaden asked.

"Hey, Kaden, Sage," one of the men said as he stepped closer. He shifted the tan Stetson back on his hair.

Evan noticed a close resemblance between Sage and the one with the tan Stetson and wondered if they were family, though he didn't have the same visceral reaction as he did with the other cowboy, Josh.

"What's up, Arthur?"

"The rest of us are going to unload the bus and carry everything to the barn or the houses. My brothers and I will take a trip on our four-by-four to see our folks," Arthur said. "You and Kaden can talk with the doctor and Charlie. I'll let Dad know what is happening with Aunt Carrie."

"Thanks, Arthur. Give Ernie our thanks for the great driving," Sage said.

Arthur tugged Sage in for a tight hug.

"Talk to you soon," Sage said. He hugged two other men.

Part of the group returned to the bus, unlocking outer compartments along with a grizzled older man, who climbed down.

"Sorry about that," Sage said to Evan.

"All of you need to do whatever you must to get comfortable. I'm sorry about altering what looks like your immediate plan of coming home and relaxing."

"We'll be fine. Let's get inside," Kaden said, wrapping his arm around Sage's waist. "Charlie?"

"Everything is ready. My Lorraine has been expecting your arrival and cooking up a storm to welcome you." Charlie he led the way to the front porch.

"Ahh, I missed her food," Kaden said as they moved with him.

Not following immediately, Evan returned to the Jeep and gathered the backpack. He carried the tablet and cell phone in his free hand. He clicked the locks with a beep.

A warm rumble of a chuckle rose behind him. "You're not from around here."

Looking away from his Jeep, Evan noticed Josh hung back. His lower body clenched against the rising heat. *What was it about this lanky cowboy?* "Pardon?"

"No one locks up around here. We're so far out, it's hard for most folks to find us. Almost everything here remains open," Josh said. "Where are you from?"

"Texas. You?"

"Born and bred in Montana. When we're not in foaling season around here, I live with my family closer to town."

"Do you work here with the others?"

"Yeah, my dad owns a store in town, but I'm not an indoors type of fella for work. I need to be under the sun and closer to nature." Stepping forward, Josh held out his hand. "I'm Joshua Holmwood, cowboy and fiddle player for our band."

Shaking hands, Evan said, "Dr. Evan Sampson, just a regular doctor." Releasing the shake, he tugged on the breast of the coat where his name was stitched.

Josh chuckled and stepped closer, almost brushing against Evan's coat. "You're a small fella for a doc."

"Size doesn't matter when it comes to medicine," Evan said, glancing up at the taller man. "It seems you're stretched out a bit."

Josh laughed.

Evan flushed at the outrageous thing. *Where the hell did my filter go?* "What's the name of the band?"

"Midnight Twang. We're starting to get a name for ourselves, a couple of hits on iTunes according to our sound and network fella, Thomas."

Several loud whinnies and pounding of multiple hooves came at them from one side of the ranch.

"Missed that. Listen to that sound," Josh said, a full smile filling his face.

Evan lifted a hand over his eyes. "What is that?"

Stepping toward the edge of the house, Josh leaned to the side. "You need to take a look at this, Doc. It's a wonderful sight not many get to see."

Curious about the sound and Josh's reaction, Evan followed him.

They were in time to see a band of horses running through the large corral, a golden stallion in the lead. Several foals followed their mothers with others around them.

"Oh wow," Evan said in a reverent whisper at the sight. "Do they belong to the stables?"

"Not quite yet, Doc, those are wild mustangs culled from one of the larger herds. Every couple of years, the government sends wranglers to cull some of the younger horses from the various bands. They offer them up for auction."

"Do the Wallstatts purchase them?"

"Every time they see some positive lines, yes."

"Are they trainable?"

"Given time, some of them can be especially the younger ones. Triple W specializes in combining mustang and quarter horse lines. They breed the best of both into the foals." Josh smiled as he watched the band turn, following the stallion. Leaning closer to assist Evan in learning about the mustangs, he pointed toward the corral with his good hand. "See the golden fella in front?"

Almost unable to concentrate upon feeling the heat rising from Josh's body and the simple scents of sweat and man, Evan blinked and focused on the horses. "Yes. Is he a stallion?"

"Yup. He's the new leader of the band. The mares follow him and are his harem. In the back will be the lesser stallions."

"The foals?"

"They're from a different leader of the herd, possibly more than one. It depends on how this group was culled from the majority. Soon as the mares come into heat, the golden will mate with them unless the Wallstatts have other plans for him."

"Continuance of the line and species."

"Yeah. Aren't they magnificent? The last of the wild ones are from the original lines of those from the Iberian horses brought to Florida and Mexico by the Spanish. Some were sold, escaped, or captured by Native Americans who adopted them as their transportation. The other wild horses run along the beaches of North Carolina's Outer Banks. One day, I'd like to travel and see them in their natural habitat," Josh said, his voice lost in his respect and adoration of the creatures. He glanced down at Evan, lowering to his lips, and back to meet Evan's gaze.

"Do you work with them?"

"I do. It's a risk and a thrill." Josh turned to Evan and smiled. "If you swing back this way, we'll show you how things work around here."

"Who's we?"

"Perhaps me," Josh said and winked. "You didn't seem shocked or disgusted by the sight of Sage and Kaden holding hands."

"Why would I be?"

"You're not offended."

"It wouldn't help being offended when I'm also gay. I didn't know many gays were out and proud up here."

"We're getting stronger and more confident of ourselves."

"You?" Evan asked, confirming his suspicions.

"Yup." Josh drawled out the popped 'P' at the end. "Hope you don't mind, but I'm dying for a taste."

"Taste—" Evan stopped when Josh lowered his head and captured Evan's lips in a soft kiss, testing the heat between them, and learning about one another. Evan found himself swept up in the kiss. *Damn, he can kiss.* A soft whimper of pleasure escaped as Josh licked along Evan's lower lip. He tilted forward, almost going off balance as Josh released their kiss. Blinking, he stared up at him. "What—"

Lifting his hand, Josh rubbed his thumb against Evan's lower lip. "Hmm. Taste delicious, Doc."

"Umm. I'm..."

Chuckling at Evan's stumbling attempt to recover, Josh gave him another wink, showing his attention and interest. "I could do that even more with you."

"Yeah. Same here," Evan said, pressing his fingers to his heated cheek. A kiss never left him so unbalanced and yearning for more.

Josh returned his attention and watched the disappearing horses.

Someone called Josh's name behind them.

They both turned to look back to the house.

"Oops," Josh said. "Charlie is yelling. We better get inside. The guys will want to speak with you more."

Turning away from the horses, Evan pointed to Josh. "May I ask about your left hand?"

Josh smiled. "Even after being kissed stupid, you remain in doctor mode."

"Habit."

"Did you check out the rest of me along with my hand?"

Evan felt his face flush.

Josh's smile widened. "I thought I felt someone checking me out. I looked back to make sure, surprised to find it was you. I'm flattered."

Evan knew the flush deepened.

"Well, I'll be, Doc. I never had this effect on a man before." Josh stepped closer, traced his finger down Evan's cheekbone. "The color is good on you. Warms your skin."

"You move a little fast," Evan teased back.

"I didn't move too much with the kiss?"

"No. Oh no. It was..."

"Wonderful for a first kiss," Josh said.

Evan nodded.

"Didn't mean to startle you, but I wanted to make my interest clear. There's not many options around here and no one interested me until I saw you being so damn considerate and gentle with Sage. You have one helluva bedside manner, Doc."

"This is a lot different than working in the ER."

"You'll cultivate better relationships with your patients here."

"Looking forward to it. How did Kaden and Sage meet?"

"They knew each other as boys. Speaking of Sage," Josh said as he stepped back. "How about we handle the problem with Sage's mama first? If you stick around, I'll tell you about my arm. I did need to call your uncle for an appointment, but you're here." He shrugged and winced. "Damn, didn't think a simple shrug would annoy my wrist. Guess I can't use my left shoulder." He rubbed his shoulder with his opposite hand and down toward his elbow.

Intrigued about Josh's obvious injury, not to mention his deep green eyes were attractive along with the rest of his whipcord lean frame, Evan couldn't help but follow him into the comfortable ranch house. He stopped by the doorway, to check out the welcoming interior. Immediately, he felt safer, more so since he entered Montana, far away from the hurt and pain in Texas.

Chapter Five

After escorting the adorable doctor inside, Josh couldn't help but check out the smaller male a little bit longer. *Oh yeah, absolutely adorable with a bubble butt. Shit, I'm sunk.* The new doctor intrigued him, even more so after their conversation. *The doc's one of the tribe. What could be better?*

"Josh. Josh..."

Josh saw Kaden snapping his fingers. He blushed and shrugged his right shoulder this time. Yeah, he had no shame while checking out the doctor, and he let Kaden know it.

Kaden shook his head. "What was the delay?"

"We saw the mustangs. Josh was nice enough to explain their presence and significance for Triple W," Evan said as he settled in an offered arm chair. He placed his tablet and phone on the coffee table.

Grumbling on the inside since he lost sight of a truly fine ass, Josh lifted an eyebrow at Kaden. Kaden shrugged and zipped his mouth closed with a finger to warn Josh to keep his mouth shut.

Sitting straighter, Sage turned to Charlie. As Josh and the others watched, hope displaced the look of sadness at the thought of the mustangs. "When did the mustangs arrive? How are they settling in?"

"Two days ago, and they're beautiful. We let them run in the western corral as we did with the other herds. A golden stallion took charge of the band."

"He remains in charge. We saw him in the lead. From what I could count, I saw six healthy foals running by their mamas." Josh glanced at the doctor, then Sage and Kaden. "I'll let all of you talk about more important things. I'm going to see what Miss Lorraine is baking in the kitchen."

"Don't leave without seeing me first," Evan said.

Turning, Josh dipped into a playful bow and air kiss. "Wouldn't think of it." He stepped back, holding a hand against his chest. "You wound me, dear Doctor, for suggesting such a horrible thing."

"Don't you dare leave me with scraps," Kaden shouted as Josh waved a hand over his head and left them to their talk.

Entering the kitchen, Josh found Charlie's wife draped in a new apron, her grayish hair piled high on her head, and her shirt sleeves rolled up past her elbows. She kneaded a pile of dough on the counter. Leaning against the frame, his violins dangling from his good hand, Josh watched her work on the bread dough until she scooped and dropped it in a prepared bowl.

"Hey there, Miss Lorraine," Josh said.

Looking over her shoulder after draping a towel over the bowl to let the dough rise, Lorraine smiled and wiped her hands on a different kitchen towel. She moved over and tugged him in a tight hug. "There you are, Josh. How was the tour?"

"Good. We got a lot of experience of performing and things we need to work on, but I think it went well. Of course, Thomas can give you all the numbers and details," Josh said as he let her take him to the table and a chair. He rested the violins and his bag on another chair.

"Want some tea or coffee?"

"A cold glass of tea would be great," he said.

Bustling about, she handed him a glass and re-filled another one for herself. When she noticed Josh's wrist, she lifted his hand carefully and brushed her fingers against the brace. "What happened to you?"

"Not sure, but it's hurting. I'm gonna see the new doc after he speaks with Sage and Kaden."

"Oh, my poor boys, such a horrible welcome home," she said, shaking her head.

"Though it hurts everyone else, it's best for Miss Carrie this is happening. She'll be back with her beloved and no longer in pain," Josh said.

"The process hurts for everyone. Didn't you want to be with them?"

"No, I don't belong there for that. I'm hanging in here until the doc is free." Josh took a long sip and sighed. "I missed this." He lowered the glass to see Lorraine studying him. "What?"

"Your eyes are brighter. Did you hit on the doc?"

Josh raised an eyebrow. "What?"

Lorraine laughed as she rose, patted his shoulder and returned to her work. "You made a good choice."

"I didn't do anything."

"Then I was mistaken when I watched you two kissing outside my window."

"Erm…"Josh felt his cheeks heat with a flush. "Kiss? What kiss?"

Turning from the stove where a large put bubbled with something smelling delicious, Lorraine waved a spoon at him and chuckled again.

The banter continued between them, passing the time until Charlie strolled into the kitchen.

"How did it go in there?" Josh asked.

"We're gonna set her up in the cabin. Both docs will be here tomorrow to set it all up. The doc is waiting for you in the living room," Charlie said as Lorraine hugged him tight, supporting one another.

"What about Sage and Kaden?"

"They went upstairs to talk. I figured they needed some time alone. Everyone else can handle the unloading. I'll leave their suitcases outside the bedroom door." Charlie tilted his head. "Go and see the doc. Don't keep him waiting."

"Yes, sir. Bye, Lorraine," Josh said as he finished the tea and scooped up his things.

"Don't you go kissing him while he's trying to figure out what's wrong," she teased him.

"Kissing? Who is kissing who now?" Charlie asked, all confused.

Josh chuckled and rushed out of the kitchen.

Entering the living room, Josh noticed Evan remained in his previous spot. This time, the doctor spoke on a phone and had a tablet opened sitting on an incline on the coffee table. Perhaps having heard him, Evan noticed him and waved him over.

Walking over, Josh settled on the end of the sofa closest to Evan. He placed the instrument cases on the cushion and waited for Evan to finish.

"Okay, Lucas, I got you. Can you see and hear me?" Evan asked, waving a hand in front of the tablet.

"Hello, all clear," a man said.

"Great. Hanging up on the phone," Evan said and closed the phone. He twisted the tablet so both of them could be captured by the camera. "Lucas, this is Joshua Holmwood, the violin player I mentioned. Josh, this is a friend and colleague of mine, Doctor Lucas Mason. He specializes in neurology and neuropathy in musicians."

"Hello, Josh, a pleasure to meet you," Lucas said with a smile.

"Hi there. Didn't expect this when I asked the doc for a quick appointment," Josh said with a chuckle.

"Once you mentioned you were a musician and a violin player, I figured your injury may involve more than tendonitis or something I could not diagnose properly. I asked Lucas to join us since this is his specialization, and it's easier than flying you to Texas," Evan said.

"Did you two work at the same place in Texas?" Josh asked them.

"We did until Evan decided to escape to an easier life in the country," Lucas said.

Josh laughed as Evan glanced away, looking a bit uncomfortable for a second.

"Anyway. Let's begin. I'm going to give Evan some instructions to examine your injury and what to look and feel. He's going to relay all the information back to me."

"Sounds good," Josh said.

"Can you remove your T-shirt? We'll need to see your entire arm. Go ahead and remove the brace."

"Not a problem," Josh said. Holding back the teasing about Evan wanting to see his chest, he reached back with his good hand and yanked the shirt over his head. He yanked the Velcro straps and slid off the brace. He tossed both toward the end of the sofa and out of their way.

Glancing over at Evan, Josh smiled when he caught Evan checking out his chest and abdomen. He wanted to flex and pose but held off.

"Hold your hand toward Doc Evan," Lucas said and gave Evan instructions on what to examine and feel.

Josh waited as Evan palpitated his fingers, hand, the wrist, and down to his elbow. Evan moved and manipulated his wrist and elbow into different positions, asking Josh what things felt like or what he experienced. Evan told Lucas his findings about the exam.

On the screen, Lucas nodded. "Okay. You're right, Evan, this sounds like a nerve issue with a possible case of tendonitis aggravating the issue. Josh, do you have your instrument?"

Josh pulled a case on his lap.

"Could you get into your position when playing? Evan, do the same exam around his hand and elbow? When he's done, I need you to play a few bars of whatever song you wish. Make sure it's something where you use those pinkie and ring fingers. I know there will be pain, but I need them to become a little aggravated to get a proper diagnosis," Lucas said.

"Not a problem," Josh said as he unlocked the case and lifted out the violin and bow. He set the case on the floor. Holding the violin between his chin and shoulder, he placed his fingers along the strings. He waited while Evan performed a similar examination of his fingers and elbow. Trying not to let the sensitive touch go straight to his cock, he held still and answered Evan about different questions.

Evan gave Lucas his findings once more. "Go ahead and play, Josh."

"Okay." Josh raised his bow and played one of the Midnight Twang's latest songs where the violin was featured more than the guitars. Before reaching the first chorus, he felt the same stinging, numbing sensation in his fingers and ache beginning. He pressed forward until he finished.

"Wow, you're a wonderful player. What's the song? Something country," Lucas said.

"I'm in a country-rock band called Midnight Twang. It's one of the latest original songs we performed on the tour," Josh said.

"You're one helluva musician," Evan said and kept Josh in the same position. "How about these fingers?"

"The numbing and tingling is stronger in them. Once I hit the first chorus, it got harder to control my dexterity and strength on the strings. If I play more songs, my wrist begins to collapse its position."

"To be expected. Lucas, you're right. There is some degree of loss of muscle strength," Evan said. "Go ahead and lower your violin."

"Thanks," Josh said and rested the violin on his lap.

"What do you think, Lucas?" Evan asked the other doctor.

"From what I'm hearing, Josh, you have a condition called ulnar nerve entrapment at your elbow. It's a nerve that runs from your neck, down around the back of your elbow, and along the ulna to the wrist. While playing the violin, your elbow is lifted in a locked position for hours at a time. This nerve has become trapped and pinched around the elbow. There isn't much tissue surrounding it. We call this cubital tunnel syndrome," Lucas said. "It's a common medical problem for many musicians due to the repetitive nature of playing music."

"So we know what it is. How can we fix it?" Josh asked.

"I would suggest several nonsurgical treatments first, but from the answers you gave Evan, I don't think they would help. You're too far along to have any benefit. I'm afraid I must recommend surgery to repair the problem."

Josh lowered his gaze and sighed hard. "What kind of surgery? How long will I be down?"

"I recommend a transposition surgery along with release. It's a combination of surgeries but would give you the most benefit. If we do your left arm, I would want to perform the same on your right arm to be safe," Lucas said. He explained the intricacies of the surgery, recovery time, and rehabilitation. "If everything goes well, about six months to a year downtime, and you can start practicing after to rebuild your muscles."

"A year?"

"At the most, but it all depends on healing and following instructions. If you push the process to fast, you'll lose the benefits of the surgery." Lucas looked at something on his desk and back at the camera lens. "What is your schedule like?"

"We finished a tour of the West Coast. The leaders said the band is taking a break for a few months. No matter what happens, I can't play like this. Can I talk this over with my family and get back with you?"

"Sure. Contact me through Evan," Lucas said. "Until then, Evan will give you some new therapies and treatments to help with the pain until the surgery."

"I've been taking ibuprofen and using heat and cold therapy. What else can I do?"

"I know a couple other ways to help lessen the pain and reduce the inflammation. They'll be better than over-the-counter medications and last longer."

"Anything to help that will be welcomed. Thank you for everything."

"More than welcome. I'm happy to help all musicians do what they love most." Lucas shifted his gaze to find Evan. "Evan, we'll talk later about details and I'll send you the list of medications. Okay?"

"Look forward to it. Thanks for being available, Lucas," Evan said.

With a wave Lucas cut off his connection.

Turning to each other, Evan placed his hand on Josh's knee. "We'll get you through this. Okay?"

Josh rubbed his finger along the edge of the violin. "I'm happy to know something is really wrong and can be fixed. What are these treatments the other doc mentioned?"

"As you've done earlier, you can continue to take ibuprofen for the pain. I'll get the other medications from Lucas and write those prescriptions for you. Before you sleep, wrap a folded towel around your elbow to keep it straight. You can secure it with medical tape."

"Are you telling me to sleep with a towel wrapped around my arm?"

"Yes. The goal is to not bend it while sleeping and keep pressure off the nerve."

"Sounds uncomfortable."

"Better than the pain and further degradation of muscle mass and the nerve itself."

While they talked, they both heard footsteps on the stairs.

"Hey? Why did we hear a violin? Josh, we told you not to play," Sage said as he entered the room. "Hey, Doc, I didn't know you were still here."

"Just finishing things up with Josh. A colleague and I requested him to play a song so we could determine the extent of his injury. My colleague was connected via the Internet and specializes in injuries in musicians," Evan said, not moving his hand from Josh's knee. "Even in pain, his playing was beautiful."

Walking over to the armchair, Sage gripped the back of it with his hands. Kaden stayed back in the doorway.

"I apologize, I didn't want Josh to overdo things, but I hoped it helped," Sage said. "Did you learn what's wrong?"

"We diagnosed a common nerve syndrome. I explained some simple treatments, but my colleague recommends surgery," Evan said. "It will fix the nerves in both of his elbows. Downtime should be around six months to a year before he can play full concerts."

"Up to a year?" Sage asked.

"I'm sorry, Sage, I let you both down. My body let you down," Josh said.

"Nonsense, Josh, you can't control how your body reacts," Kaden said, entering the room to make his point.

"When will this surgery happen?"

"Josh wants to discuss things with his family." Evan gathered his things and repacked his bag. "I need to get going onto the rest of my appointments."

"Thank you for everything," Sage said and stepped away with Kaden.

Stepping over to Evan, Josh remained bare chested, supporting his left hand. "Must you leave?"

"I can't stop visiting other patients on my first day of house calls. I'll be back around," Evan said. "Call when you make your decision."

Rising with Evan, Josh walked him to the front door. "What if I want to ask you to dinner?"

A soft flush covered Evan's cheeks. Evan poked his hand inside the bag and tugged out a card and pen. He flipped the card over, scratched out a number, and held it out. "My personal line."

"Really?"

Evan nodded with a smile as he clipped the pen to his shirt pocket. He traced his fingers along Josh's cheekbone and patted his bare chest. "Anytime. I need to go. You're allowed to put your shirt back on."

Reluctant to let him out of his sight, Josh captured Evan's mouth in a light kiss. "You don't like me without a shirt?"

"Oh, you're a strong distraction."

"Which means you'll remember me." Josh winked and smiled. "Take care."

"I will," Evan said and walked away to his Jeep. As he drove away, he waved a hand which Josh returned.

"Impressive. You move fast."

Spinning at the teasing voice, Josh found a smiling Kaden standing behind him. "I umm...I..." He was saved by his phone ringing. Yanking it out, he answered it before checking the number. "Hello, this is Josh."

"Where are you?"

At the gruff voice, Josh straightened his back. "Dad. Hi. I'm back at the Triple W."

"Get your butt over here. Now."

"Dad—"

"Now."

Leaning away when the phone clicked off, Josh stared at the phone. "That was strange."

"Are you okay?" Kaden asked.

"It was my dad. I have to go home and see what's wrong. I'll call you guys later. Okay?"

"Sure. Good to hear you have a diagnosis," Kaden said and tugged Josh into a light hug.

Returning the hug, Josh rushed back inside, yanked on his T-shirt and gathered his bag and violin cases. He wound his way to his battered Ford F-150. Leaving his duffel and cases in the cab, he headed to the music barn where they practiced and recorded. There he found his pair of suitcases along with others from the band. He grabbed both of them and saw their electronics fella, Thomas, working in his area.

"Hey, Thomas, got a call from home. Gotta run. See ya later," Josh called out. He knew Thomas heard him when the other man waved.

Returning to his truck, he placed the suitcases in the back, climbed inside the cab, and drove away from the Triple W. The last thing in his rear-view mirror was the racing mustangs.

Chapter Six

It didn't take long for Josh to learn he would no longer be welcome in his parents' home. The moment he stepped inside, his father tossed a packet of envelopes and letters at him.

As the papers fell to the floor, Josh stared down at them. He saw the writing, and it cut straight to his heart. His former boyfriend and first love, Stephen, wrote those letters after he escaped Montana for a California university. Only, for some damn reason, as if he had to prove he was a man to his father, Stephen joined the Marines. Instead of coming home a hero and Josh's love, Stephen returned to Montana in a box. Those letters were the last piece he had to remember his time with Stephen, his first love.

Lifting his gaze, Josh glared at his father. "Where did you find those?"

"Does it matter?"

"I'm a little old for you to dig through my personal belongings."

"Damn glad I did. I found out what you were hiding from me all this damn time."

"What would that be?"

"You're a faggot. How the hell did I raise a faggot?" his father shouted, holding a hand up to stop his wife from protesting.

His good hand clenched in a fist as the anger rose at his father's hateful words, but Josh forced himself to release the tension from his hand. "Dad, I'm still the same son you raised and knew before you found those letters."

"Like hell I do. I don't know anything about you." His father pointed a hand to the scattered letters. "What is the meaning of those? Who the hell is Stephen?"

"Someone I knew. Someone I loved."

"Do you still feel that way?" His father stepped closer into Josh's personal bubble. He glared at him, narrowing his gaze. "Are you a faggot? TELL ME!"

Holding back a flinch at the scream, Josh stood firm. "Yes, I'm gay. Are you happy?" He held still as he spoke the truth, unable to say anything else. In his heart he knew this moment eventually would occur. "I'm proud of it, and I'm not hiding who I am. I never hid who I am. You never wanted to see the truth."

His father cracked the back of his hand across Josh's face. "You lied!"

Josh's eyes watered as he dropped back a few steps. His cheek and face were on fire from the intense hit.

"You're no son of mine." His father pointed a finger at the door. "Get your ass to that dump over the garage, clean it out, and leave. You're never to return or speak to anyone in this home."

Josh gathered the precious letters. He escaped before his anger unleashed in the worst way. Leaving, he raced to the simple apartment above the garage. Stepping inside, he stared at the destruction his father caused. Personal items scattered the floor, most ruined by the careless actions. Others could be salvaged.

Leaning back against the door, Josh closed his eyes and screamed his anger. He slammed his good fist against the solid wood.

Returning to the Triple W, Josh recognized this was what Kaden went through leaving his family behind. Now it seemed it would be his turn. Pulling by the main house, Josh got out.

Sage and Kaden walked outside around the same moment, talking to one another. Sage looked up first and held out his arm to stop Kaden, who looked around and spotted Josh leaning against his truck.

"Josh, what's happening?" Sage climbed down the steps and walked toward him.

"Do you have room for another lost soul?" Josh asked.

"What?"

"My father kicked me out. He ransacked my place for some damn reason and found the letters from Stephen. He went ballistic," Josh said.

"Cut from the same cloth as my father," Kaden said as he followed Sage. He placed a hand on Josh's shoulder.

"Hopefully, mine won't turn as violent as yours." Josh winced. "Sorry."

"No, don't be, it's what happened. I'm sure what he did affected everyone. He's where he belongs behind those bars." Kaden tugged Josh against him, holding him tight.

Josh accepted the hug and comfort from someone who knew exactly what he was going through. "Thanks, K."

"Welcome, J-man." Kaden looked back at Sage. "We can make room for another lost soul."

"He can join the others. We're a ranch and family full of lost souls needing a safe welcoming place," Sage said with a smile. "Welcome to the family, completely this time. This is your home, and you'll never be turned away, Joshua."

Josh gave them a watery smile. "I'll head to the bunkhouse and chose a place."

"Nah," Sage said and waved a hand to dismiss the idea. He nodded toward the house. "Take one of the suites in the main house. There's more than enough room."

"Are you sure?"

"Yeah, it's Kaden, me, and Charlie with his wife. Plenty of room," Sage said.

"Just not too close to the master suite," Kaden said, wiggling his eyebrows.

Josh laughed at Kaden's obvious point as Sage blushed hard. "Not even going to touch that," he said when he got his breath back from laughing so hard.

"Idiot," Sage said and jabbed his elbow in Kaden's stomach. "Help him unload his stuff, you idiot."

"What? Me?" Kaden asked, all innocently.

Sage glared at him until Kaden held up his hands and rushed over to the truck.

"Apparently, I'm supposed to help you, or I'm in the doghouse," Kaden said.

Josh continued to chuckle at their antics. Part of him desired to have the same feelings and connection with a man of his own. He thought it would have been Stephen, until their lives went different directions.

"Besides, I don't want you to strain that wrist any further," Sage said as he appeared next to them, tugging boxes toward him. "We know what's wrong with it, but that doesn't mean you should overdo things."

"I got swept into things with the doc and forgot to even ask. What's happening with your mama?"

"According to the doc, the cancer is so advanced there's not much more they can do. They're going to make her comfortable in the cabin with Aunt Patti," Sage said.

"Cancer sucks."

"So does Alzheimer's."

Josh gripped Sage's arm with his good hand in a show of support. "Is the doc coming back?"

"He's planning on coming back tomorrow or the next day with everything they need to support her. His uncle will probably be with him to help set up things along with a nurse. Don't know how this will all go over with Mama, but there isn't much choice now."

"What about your sister and brother? Did you tell them?"

"I called Rose. Since Basil doesn't contact us much whether he's deployed or on base wherever in the world, I sent an email to contact me and also asked the American Red Cross to relay a message to his command. I don't know how often he can access his email, or if he would bother to contact me back."

"Things are still broken between you."

"Yes, he never called me about the letter from the bank. I don't think he wants anything to do with Montana." Sage rubbed the back of his neck while he kicked a loose rock with his boot. "Damn stubborn bastard."

"Just like the rest of the family," Josh said with a grin.

"Oh no, he's worse. He's just like Dad from the attitude to those big blue eyes. They're a pair." Sage kicked another rock to follow the first one. "Even if they both come home, we'll have to wait for the right time to see her. I don't want to upset Mama."

"You mentioned Basil had a huge row with your dad."

"They had the argument about his signing up for service." Sage shook his head. "If it was something deeper, I don't know. All I know is Basil gathered a couple of things in a backpack and left. He hasn't been back since."

"Not even for leave?"

"He goes somewhere else."

"Damn. That's just wrong."

"It's Basil. As a helicopter pilot, I'm sure he's been in the thick of action in Afghanistan, Iraq, and the search for terrorists. Not sure why he moved to the embassy," Sage said.

"Hopefully, he'll make the decision to come home and let this land heal him," Josh said.

"That's the hope."

While they talked and gathered what Josh could salvage from the destruction of his rooms, Sage led them through the house. They went upstairs, and Josh chose a suite to look over the corral holding the mustangs. Sage and Kaden lowered their burdens on the floor and let Josh do the rest.

"Call if you need any help," Kaden said.

"Where are you two going?"

"Checking out the mustangs."

"I still want to work with them."

"How can you work with a wild mustang?"

"Peppermints, a lead line, and my voice in the training circle. It works with most of them. I learned from Sage's dad," Josh said with a grin at Sage, who nodded.

"Next to Dad and me, Josh is the best with the wild ones. He can break most of them to the halter and training without ruining their spirit. Of course there may be one or two that don't want anything to do with humans, but he can bring them around with time." Sage looked at Josh. "We'll work together with them. Don't do it alone."

"I promise. Nothing major until things get fixed. I'll think about the surgery, but it looks like there's no other options. I'll take a look online at the syndrome to learn more."

"Good. Dinner is in two hours. I'll tell Lorraine to expect you," Sage said.

"Thanks again for letting me stay."

"You're home. You're family. Nothing more. Nothing less. Settle in and get some rest before dinner," Sage said and left with Kaden.

Josh sat down on the bed, looked around at his pitiful pile of belongings and around the comfortable bedroom. It was connected to a decent bathroom and sitting area. Rising again, he walked to the back windows and twitched back the curtains. He smiled when he watched the golden mustang leading his harem through another run of the corral while they got used to their surroundings and cautiously lowered their heads to chomp the nutritious, rich grass. The foals nudged their mamas, wanting their own meals. Leaning against the window, Josh forgot about unpacking and time as he watched the horses.

Halfway through the following morning, regular chores and work at the ranch continued as if they never went away on tour. The heat of the sun poured down over Josh and the other cowboys working the ranch.

Standing in the small training circle, Josh stayed relaxed with all his concentration on the dancing golden mustang. He selected the harem leader as always since the others would follow his lead. He wanted to check out how much spirit and determination were in the horse. If things didn't progress well today, he made the decision to move onto the younger stallions to see which ones had promise.

While the mustang's golden coat glimmered under the sun, the tell-tale dark strip along his back split the color. Josh felt like he was melting. The ancient gray Stetson pulled down low provided some shade but not much. His boots were dusty along with the faded jeans. He wore a white T-shirt, soaked along his back and front with sweat. Over the T-shirt, he wore a light-weight, button-down shirt, buttoned along the bottom to prevent it flapping around and scaring the animal. Since he was working with the horse, he decided to wrap the brace around his sore wrist. Tugging out the blue handkerchief, Josh wiped the sweat off the back of his neck and his forehead.

The mustang continued to dance, tossing his head, whinnying to his harem, and not paying much attention to the human.

"Yeah, I know, you're a proud fella and don't give a shit about me, but you're gonna wanna pay attention soon, golden boy," Josh whispered.

Stepping back with care to the fence, Josh grabbed the bottle of water he left. He popped the top and gulped several swallows. Leaning forward, he squeezed more cold water along his neck.

"This one is being a stubborn mule." Charlie rested his boot along the lowest rung, leaning over the top rail as he watched the give and take between horse and man. Sage, Kaden, and Thomas stood near him.

"He's warier than the others, that's for sure. I'm giving him time to listen to my voice, learn my scent and what he can get away with," Josh said. "He'll come around in time."

"Should we move to the younger stallions later today or tomorrow? See if we can pull them away and work with them?" Sage suggested.

"I was thinking the same thing. Let this fella see we're not hurting anyone in his band. He may listen to us a little better."

"Which one would you want next?"

"Thinking the painted one that runs at the back."

"Same here. Seems more placid and easygoing."

"I think he's on the bottom rung of the ladder. We could train him up to be an excellent, reliable ranch or rodeo horse."

"Not the lines I want for breeding," Sage said.

"Snip snip?"

"Yup."

Chuckling softly, Josh took another few gulps of water and handed the bottle back to Charlie. "If this one doesn't cooperate, I'm gonna give him the *snip snip*."

Sage chuckled back.

On the other side of them, Kaden and Thomas winced and adjusted their stance to protect their manhood.

"Hey, watch the talk about those scissors, fellas," Thomas said.

Listening to their antics with half a mind, Josh returned his full attention back to the horse. Clicking softly and using low encouraging words, he dug into his shirt pocket and held a peppermint candy on the palm of his glove. He held the hand flat toward the snorting, dancing mustang.

Not quite sure what to do, the mustang pawed a hoof along the ground, whinnied, and tossed his head and elegant mane. Flicking his tail, he stepped forward, stretching out his neck to sniff at Josh's hand.

"Come on, pretty boy, it's a treat," Josh urged the stallion.

Snorting, blowing hot air over Josh's glove and lower arm, the stallion sniffed again. He lipped the treat from the glove.

"There you go, how about that? Not bad, huh?" Josh continuing to talk in his low voice. He held out his hand, keeping the coiled lead rope in his other hand against his leg.

The stallion finished with the treat and sniffed Josh's hand. He smelled the remnants of the candy, but nothing more.

With a smile, Josh stroked the soft nose. He moved his hand down the elegant face and lean neck. He patted the stallion's neck, continuing with the encouragement. Moving his hand with the rope, he slid it around the horse's skin, letting him get the feel of it.

"Nothing to fear, pretty boy, nothing at all. Only kindness, I promise," Josh said as he worked with the horse.

It took another long, hot hour, but finally, Josh slipped the makeshift rope halter around the horse's nose and head. The stallion whinnied, tossed his head, and danced away from Josh. He shook his head and mane as he got used to the sensation.

Stepping away, not pushing the jittery stallion, Josh returned to the fence. He accepted the bottle of water for another long sip of the cool water one of the guys replenished for him. He nodded to Simon, who wandered over to watch the progress with the others.

"Damn, he's a beauty," Sage said.

"Perfect coloring to go with some of the mares," Josh said. "Imagine the foals you'll get from this fella if he stops being stubborn."

"I can't wait. Hopefully, we can start breeding him for the spring foaling season," Sage said.

"He's a crafty one. Definitely a smart one. I can see it in his eyes," Josh said. Leaning forward, he squeezed more water on his neck. "Damn, it's hot out here. What's it hitting on the thermometer?"

"Almost ninety-two," Kaden said. "How much longer do you want to work with him?"

"I'll leave it up to him," Josh said.

The rumbling of several vehicles on the pot-holed road alerted everyone to newcomers. Josh glanced away from the stallion and caught sight of the bright magnet on the Jeep's side. The new doc was back.

With a grin he whistled low to the stallion as he walked closer, holding out several peppermints. Moving closer, he took hold of the halter and attached a lead rope. The stallion twisted and tugged, pulling away as Josh released some of the line. He tugged back toward the end, showing the stallion who was in charge of this little dance.

A loud backfire cracked through the quiet. The mustang reared on his hind legs, pawing the air with his front hoofs, whinnying loud and shrill, terrified.

"Whoa. Easy, boy, easy." Grabbing onto the rope with both hands, Josh tried to control the rearing.

The horse wouldn't have anything to do with him.

Twisting as he came down on four hooves, the stallion bucked and kicked into a hard gallop. He headed straight toward Josh and the fence. Unable to get out of the way, Josh screamed when his bad wrist got caught between the horse and the edge of the fence post. He felt something crunch and twist deep inside, the brace offering no protection whatsoever from the thousand-plus animal.

With another deep whinny, the stallion galloped to the far side. He kicked his back legs against the railing, ready to snap the wood for freedom.

"Get him out of here! Before he destroys the corral, get him out," Josh shouted as he slid to the ground. Deep in pain, Josh cradled his left hand close to his body. From the odd angle of his hand and wrist, he knew he was in deep shit. Things were definitely broken inside.

In response to his orders, Charlie worked both gates to shift the stallion to the larger corral. As the mustang swept passed him, Charlie managed to unhitch and release the rope. Freed from the corral and rope, the golden stallion raced away.

"Joshua!" Sage shouted.

Darkness filled his vision, but Josh forced himself to stay grounded and fight the urge to let the blackness swept over him. He needed to keep aware of what was happening. Hell, as a cowboy for most of his life, he'd had far more painful injuries.

Licking his lower lip, Josh concentrated on pulling in deep breaths through his nose and blowing out from his mouth. Pain continued to wrack him, firing from his ruined hand, and caused tears to sting his eyes. Controlling his breathing again, pushing down the panic attack, Josh managed to stay aware.

With the corral empty and safe, Sage, Kaden and Simon vaulted the fence and raced to his side. Thomas remained on the other side, holding back the others from helping out and getting in the way.

"Fuuuuuuck. This hurts," Josh said as Sage and Kaden dropped next to him.

"No shit," Sage said.

"How many times have we told you to move your ass?" Simon teased.

"I know. I know," Josh said and clenched his jaw as another wave of pain rolled through him. "Shit..."

"Take care of the equipment and Miss Carolyn, Uncle Alfred. I can handle this," Evan shouted.

Happy to see his doctor racing around the corral to the gate, Josh focused on Evan. He watched until Evan crouched next to him.

"Hey Doc, how ya been?" Josh asked, his words started slurring a bit as he continued to concentrate on his breathing and blocking the intense pain.

"What did you do to yourself now?" Evan said, keeping his voice light and teasing.

"Got it squished between a horse and fence," Josh said, closing his eyes to rest.

"Josh, Joshua, open your eyes," Sage said, resting his hand on Josh's shoulder.

Tilting his head to find Sage, Josh could no longer hide the tears. "It's my fucking string hand. The same damn hand."

"We'll get it fixed. Stay with us," Sage said.

"You know I can help you," Evan said as he pulled out different equipment from his bag. He gently palpitated Josh's hand with a tender care.

"Ouch," Josh said.

"I know. Ssh, hang in there," Evan said as he concentrated on the break. "Okay. We can't handle this out here or the clinic. I need to get you to Kalispell."

"Kalispell?" Sage asked.

"Closest hospital with all the services we need to fix his hand properly. I don't want him to lose the ability to play," Evan explained.

"What about his other surgery?"

"Looks like it just moved up in the timeline. I'll call and ask Lucas if he can fly north to perform the surgery. Damn, I'll need to get his presence cleared with the hospital board. Shit," Evan said and waved a hand. "Don't worry. I'll figure out the details."

"Umm. Over here. The man with the broken hand is in pain," Josh said, getting a word between them. "Could use a little more help with the pain, Doc."

"I haven't forgotten you. You broke more than your hand. I'll give you a shot in the Jeep." Evan wrapped thick cotton around Josh's swollen, pain-filled arm from his elbow to his fingers. He added a temporary brace on top and bottom. Using an Ace bandage and Sage's help, he covered everything with several wraps and secured everything. "Okay. Sage, get on the other side. Kaden, I'll need you at his front to support him. Josh, we need to get you on your feet and to the Jeep. I'll support your arm to make sure it doesn't get jostled. Okay?"

Josh nodded.

"Simon, clear the way and make sure we have room. Charlie, could you get a fast backpack of Josh's things including his wallet? Toss it in the Jeep," Evan said.

"Will do," Charlie said as he waved everyone out of the way as he jogged toward house and hollered for Lorraine.

"On three, guys," Evan said and counted down.

Josh made a high keening noise as he pushed to his feet with help. The pain level increased. Breathing through it, he stared at Evan, using his face to ground him.

Evan moved his hands to support Josh's arm. "Okay?"

"Yeah. Get me outta here."

"Working on it." Evan looked at the others. "Move steady and easy to the Jeep. Head to the passenger side around the back."

Biting his lower lip, Josh let the men support and walk him out of the corral and across the main lot. Between Simon and Thomas, the others stayed back as they kept on course for the Jeep. They reached Evan's Jeep and went around the far side to the passenger seat. Kaden opened the door while Sage supported Josh. Evan rushed to the back, grabbed several blankets and folded them into a cushioning pillow. He placed them against the seat and motioned for Sage to move Josh closer. Taking over, he assisted Josh climbing into the seat and positioned his arm on the makeshift pillow. He tucked another blanket pillow between Josh's belly and arm and a third supported underneath.

"Comfortable?"

"Much as I can be," Josh said as he leaned back against the seat.

"Good. Let me belt you in," Evan said as he dragged the seatbelt around him, leaning over Josh's lap and clicked it in place.

Wishing he wasn't in so much damn pain to enjoy the feeling of Evan's body against him, Josh closed his eyes.

Kaden raced away and returned with Evan's bag. "Figured you would need this."

"I do, thanks," Evan said and rustled through the bag. He held a syringe and glass bottle of fluid. Sticking the needle in the top, he drew out the fluid and tapped the barrel with his fingers to remove bubbles. "I'm giving you a shot of morphine, Josh. It'll help you during the trip."

Josh nodded and barely flinched at the needle poke. He closed his eyes and let out a long breath.

"Here's his bag," Lorraine said, getting Josh's attention. He watched her hand over his backpack to Evan before turning to him. "Oh, you poor dear."

Tilting his head, Josh looked over at Lorraine and gave her a soft smile. "I'm in good hands. Doc will fix me up."

"We'll come and be with you. You're not alone."

"Thanks, Miz Lorraine," Josh said and felt his eyelids get heavier. "What was in that shot, Doc?"

"A little of this and a little of that," Evan said as he closed the door.

Never one to really handle pain medications all too well, Josh enjoyed the almost psychedelic displacement in his head. He heard the rest of his muffled talk with his new family, a family who truly cared about him.

"I'll get him to Kalispell and worked on. Once I know answers, and he's settled in a room, I'll call everyone. My uncle is here to help get Miss Carolyn all set up with the new equipment, nurse, and instructions," Evan said. "I'm sure he also yelled at the truck driver to get the damn engine fixed."

"Take care of him for us," Sage said, placing his palm against the window.

Josh used his good hand to lift a finger and tap the glass back.

"It's a promise," Evan said as he walked around and climbed into the driver's seat. He waved toward the others across Josh's body and turned the engine on to pull away.

"On to Kalispell?" Josh asked, his voice a little slurred from the medications.

"Yes. Close your eyes. Try to rest."

It was the last thing Josh heard as his eyes closed.

Over the next week, Josh was in and out of awareness of what was happening around him. He knew he remained in the Kalispell hospital in a room by himself other than the nurses and doctors. He remembered talking to his friends who stayed at various times to care for him and the ranch. Doc Evan visited him daily, staying to speak with him, especially during the evenings. The last two days, he didn't remember much other than being taken in for surgery.

With a yawn and soft moan, he woke to face another day. His mind wasn't as fuzzy that morning. Hearing soft blips, beeps, and scratches, he enjoyed the comforting sound of the machines. Opening his eyes, he saw a nurse walking in, checking his vitals, and administering medication to the IV in his hand. He didn't move until she left him alone.

Grumbling, he took stock of what was happening around him. The damn tube remained shoved up his cock. Another plastic thingie pushing oxygen into his nose bothered the ever-living hell out of him. He wanted to scratch the pinch in his hand where they placed the IV needle, but he couldn't move either arm.

Then he felt something heavy weighing down his left arm. It felt completely immobile with an annoying twitchy itching sensation. Pulling in fresh oxygen, he looked down and saw a thick, white cast covering his left arm from the shoulder to his fingers. It kept his arm bent at a gentle angle. He blinked at the crazy sight. His right arm wasn't much better with a thick bandage wrapped from mid-biceps to mid-forearm, that elbow also kept at a gentle angle.

"What the hell?"

Chapter Eight

Hoping to find Josh more lucid, Evan entered the room with a tablet held under one arm. Due to hospital policy, he wore pressed charcoal trousers, dove gray dress shirt, and a complementing tie under his pristine white doctor's coat. His stethoscope was pushed into one pocket, a random assortment of pens clipped to a breast pocket. Thanks to his uncle, he also had his image on an official badge.

"Don't you look all professional," Josh said.

Chuckling at Josh's comment, Evan smiled when he saw Josh awake in the bed, struggling to adjust his position in the bed. "There's that teasing flirtatious fellow."

Stopping his fussing around, Josh gifted him with a warm inviting smile. Then a curious look appeared in his gaze. "Flirtatious?"

Evan raised an eyebrow. *Now this is an interesting situation. Flirt boy doesn't remember a thing. Definitely can't tolerate the higher pain medication.* "You've hit on me and flirted your ass off with me and, I heard, every male nurse, over the last few days not once but multiple times in any duration of time. Your friends were laughing their asses off to the point some of them left to continue cracking up outside."

"Ermm..."

"Don't remember a thing, do you?"

Josh shook his head.

"Well, you were under the influence. In a fashion," Evan said with a wink. "None of us realized the flirt came out of you while you were high on pain meds."

"Hmm. Under the influence without the hangover. Not bad." Josh flushed hard. "Should I say I'm sorry?"

"Don't be. I enjoyed every bit of it," Evan said as he walked closer and set the tablet down on the pushed-aside tray. He settled on the edge of the bed and tapped his finger to the tip of Josh's nose. Leaning closer, he lowered his tone to an intimate level. "I'm thrilled to be on the receiving end of a gorgeous flirt. It's been a while for me."

"With your looks. Nah. Don't believe it."

Sitting back, Evan lowered his gaze to the bed. The pain from Texas clenched his heart. He needed to get this block out of their way for any type of future. "I was in a relationship in Texas. As always, he was the perfect gentleman in the beginning, but later…" He trailed off, still unable to say the words.

"Did he hurt you?"

Evan's breath hitched as Josh nailed the problem on the head. He lifted his gaze to connect with Josh's stare. "Broke my heart, pride, and self-respect. I'm working on building them back. Your undeniable attraction to me is helping boost my confidence. Thank you."

"I promise to never break your heart." Josh's nose wiggled, and he jerked his head, rubbing his ear against his shoulder. "Dang it."

"What happened?"

"Itch. Bad…ear…help…"

Laughing, Evan scratched his fingers around Josh's ear and lower head. He tangled his fingers in Josh's hair, twirling a few locks around his fingers. He gave a few gentle tugs, and Josh moaned with pleasure. "Hmm. Looks like a nurse gave you a bath. Your hair is soft, smells clean, a bit like tea tree oil."

"One of the volunteers washed and dried my hair yesterday. I was a little awake for it, but it was a girl. No fun." Josh blew out a raspberry of displeasure.

Evan chuckled and their gaze met, heated.

Josh wiggled and winced.

Concerned, Evan pressed his hand on Josh's shoulder. "What is it now?"

"Erection and catheter don't like one another," Josh said.

"Oh, shit, I'm sorry. There's no way you can get up and take care of personal things, so we kept it in."

"Yeah, yeah. Bugger it all."

"Guess we better stop for now." Evan rose from the bed, tugged the visitor's chair closer and sat down. "Other than the issue with the catheter, how are you doing? Are you in any discomfort or pain?"

"No, the nurse was here and added something to the IV."

Evan pulled the tray closer and tapped on the tablet. He swiped the screen. "That was a light pain killer, nothing strong since you can't handle them, but I wanted to make sure you were kept comfortable."

Josh tilted his head toward the shoulder-high cast and his other wrapped arm. "Does this look a little comfortable to you? I feel like I'm in a straight-jacket and can't move for shit."

"Got an itch?"

"Hell yes, right down the back of my arm above the elbow. Same for both damn arms."

"It's to be expected since that's where the incision ends," Evan said. "Lucas was pleased with the results though."

"What the hell happened? Doc Lucas was here?"

"Do you want to know everything since we left the ranch or arrived at the hospital?"

"Whatever gets me the full story."

Evan chuckled. "Haven't lost your flirtatious mood or humor. Good to see."

"Tell me, Doc."

"Okay. Okay." Evan held up a hand to stop Josh's interruptions. "Thanks to several X-rays, an orthopedist and I discovered several bones broken in your hand, both wrist bones were fractured, and something called an extra-articular fracture of the radius that displaced. Basically, your radius bone looked like this—" Evan lifted his hands in position to show how the bones were out of alignment. "The ligaments and tendons were fine, which is good news."

"Is all of this bad?"

"Not really. Bones will heal and be strong. Damaged ligaments are harder to heal. Even with the broken bones, it'll take a couple of months before you can resume light activities and around three to six months until more vigorous activity. You can use physical therapy to strengthen the muscles and flexibility, but you can't practice until nine months out at least. We don't want a setback. You'll have some weakness and stiffness for another year, maybe two, but you can play full time."

"Okay. That takes care of part of the problem. What's the other half?"

"I'm getting there. Once I explained you were a prominent musician playing the violin, the orthopedist elected to perform surgery to align and secure the bones so they would heal straight and sure for you. At the same time, I figured we should take care of your original surgery."

"The one with the trapped nerves."

"Yes. I asked Lucas to fly north to perform the surgery at the same time. I didn't trust anyone else to help you. It took a couple of days to get hospital acceptance and privileges for Lucas, but I managed to push everything through with my uncle's help and giving out a few favors. Lucas flew here and worked with the orthopedist. Neither one wanted your left arm and hand moved to disturb the healing, so they chose to cast to your shoulder. Once the stitches are ready to come out, they'll cut it off, take out the stitches, and re-cast you to mid-forearm until the bones are healed. The rest will have a lighter bandage. The other arm only required the bandaging until it's time for the stitches to be removed, and a lighter bandage will replace it."

"How am I supposed to get dressed? Hell, I can't bend shit. I can't even scratch my balls."

Evan swallowed a chuckle. "I'm sure you can find help with that issue."

"Which one? Dressing me or scratching my balls."

"Which do you prefer I help with?"

Josh grinned and waggled an eyebrow. "Which one are you offering to help me with?"

"I'm pretty sure we both know the answer to that one."

Another grin cracked Josh's face, but he shook his head for a second.

"Okay?"

"A little loopy but good." He yawned for a second. "Do you give sponge baths?"

Evan chuckled not holding it back that time. "You're incorrigible."

"You like me."

"Hmm, you seem to be growing on me."

"It that the only thing growing?"

"And there's the flirt on pain meds," Evan said.

Josh yawned, longer this time.

"I should go and let you sleep."

"All I've been doing is sleeping."

"Sleeping allows your body to heal."

"Yeah. Yeah." Focusing his sleep-heavy eyes on Evan, Josh asked, "Where's Sage and Kaden?"

"They stayed with you and left a couple of hours ago to return to the ranch."

"Is mustang okay?"

Evan straightened and raised an eyebrow. "Why do you ask?"

"He didn't know what was happening. The backfire scared him. Unknown environment. Not his fault," Josh mumbled. He moved his right hand but cursed.

"What is it? What can I help with?"

"This fricking sucks. I can't even control the damn bed."

"I can help with that part. It's not for a long time. Only until things heal internally." Rising, Evan found the controller for the bed. Holding it in his hand, he pressed the button to lift the head into a gentle incline. "How is that? Better?"

"Yeah, anything other than lying flat on my back." Josh tilted his head to look at Evan.

"It'll get better. This is the roughest part," Evan said, trailing his fingers down Josh's cheek.

"Don't leave me. Please."

"I need to leave for a couple of rounds to see patients, but I'll return."

"Stay with me?"

"Not now, I will later. I promise."

Josh closed his eyes and turned away from Evan.

Concerned about Josh's reaction, Evan rested his hands on the bed and leaned over him. "Where's your family, Josh? What about your parents? I can call them for you."

"No one would give a damn. They kicked me out."

"What?"

"My father found the letters I exchanged with my first boyfriend. He didn't appreciate knowing his son was a homosexual."

"When did this happen?"

"Same day I came home with the band and we met. Sage and Kaden took me in. They're my family now."

Resting his fingers on Josh's chin, Evan gently turned Josh's face back. He studied him, looking deep into the sleepy gaze. "You're not alone to deal with this. Okay? As much as I want to stay with you, I'm a doctor at the same time. I can't turn away from my duties."

Josh blinked, tears brimming his eyes.

"Ssh," Evan said, moving his hand to brush his fingers through Josh's hair. "I promise, you're not going to be alone. All of us will figure out how to help you best."

"All of us?"

"Sage, Kaden, Charlie, the band, and me. We're all invested in your well-being. They've all been in and out, staying with you, throughout the last week. I asked and Kaden said they created a schedule to make sure you weren't alone for long. I believe they mentioned someone called Thomas and Simon would be here next."

"Thomas is our tech guy. Simon plays the mandolin, slide guitar, and banjo. Good fellas."

"Then I can leave you in good hands while I work. Let the nap take over and sleep. When you wake, your friends will be here and hopefully a decent meal."

"No green Jell-O."

Evan chuckled. "Sorry. Mandatory for every patient. But I think they server the red cherry one at this hospital." He leaned closer and brushed his lips against Josh's mouth.

He felt Josh respond in a lazy way. When Josh wiggled under him, Evan leaned back and realized Josh wanted to wrap his arms around him, but his arms wouldn't cooperate.

"Ssh. Rest. We'll hold each other soon. I'll see you later," Evan said. He placed another kiss on Josh's mouth and let him sleep.

Returning to the hospital after a full day of visiting patients at their homes and in the clinic, Evan didn't mind the long drive back to Kalispell. There was something special waiting back in a hospital room. A gorgeous something special with a lean body thanks to years spent on horseback and topped off with deep green eyes and caramel-colored hair. Evan smiled at how he enjoyed snacking on caramel candies.

Whistling to himself as he walked the hallway to Josh's room, he paused near the nurses' station. He heard singing, albeit a little off key and loopy, but it was singing. Next to him, the nurses were chuckling.

"What happened? Is that my patient?"

The head nurse nodded and chuckled again. "Your patient rolled in his sleep and whacked his casted hand and arm against the rails. He shouted and cried out in pain, curling around it."

Evan blanched as his mouth dropped. "Why the hell didn't anyone call me?"

"I called the orthopedic surgeon and he ordered a dose of Vicodin. I applied the dosage to his IV needle."

"What? He's my patient now. I control his medication," Evan said and dragged a hand through his hair. "Oh, shit, this one can't handle the harder drugs."

"I noticed."

Raucous laughter rolled through the hallway.

"And that?"

"It seems most of his band members are with him. I didn't know he was in a band," the nurse said.

"He's the violin player for Midnight Twang." Evan shook his head. "Looks like I'm in for a long night with them."

"I apologize, Doctor, I should have checked with you. Though, I must say he's adorably cute and loopy when he's high on pain medication."

Evan waved his hand. "Next time, I get called first. No matter how little of a problem. Okay?"

"Yes, Doctor."

"I'll go check on them," he said and walked down the hallway.

"Did you see the fine ass on my doc? It the best...Ya know I love you guys. Always love...love...love..." Josh trailed off as he sang the word and turned it into the famous Beatles' lyrics. "Everybody with me..."

His friends cracked up laughing as they joined in on the lyrics to appease their inebriated friend.

"Went from my ass, to country, to the Beatles. Interesting loop of conversation." Reaching the doorway, he stayed just out of sight to check out the room. He discovered his loopy patient surrounded by his band mates and brothers, the same group which left the bus.

Things shifted from laughing to Josh sniffling, crocodile tears welling and falling down his cheeks. "What am I gonna do? I wanna love on him. How can I get him to notice the little old fiddle player? I'm not in the front of the band. I'm…" The area between his eyebrows and forehead scrunched up. "Back-up. Ick."

"You already smashed your hand," someone responded. "What else can you do?"

"Could whack my cast again…but that fucking hurts."

"Which is how you got in this state."

"Love…Love…Love…Dah da dadummmm…Me and the doc…Love…Love…Love…" Josh went off in another direction from the sappy, whiny self.

Pressing his fist against his mouth to hold back the laughter, Evan cleared his throat and stepped around the doorway.

"Ahh. Lookee. Lookee." Josh struggled to raise his right arm to point. "There he is. The love of my life! My savior. The fabulous doctor."

His band mates cracked up laughing.

While he shook his head, Evan entered the room, closing the door so the other patients wouldn't be disturbed. He crossed the room, folded his arms over his chest, and stared from one member to the next and ended with Josh. "What's going on around here?"

"Oooh, doc, can ya fix my achy breaky heart? It hurts so…" Josh said to the others immense pleasure and laughter.

"Oh shit, he's pulling out the bad nineties music of Cyrus. Someone save us," one of the guys sitting on the floor said. He held his hands in the air as if praying to God. "Anything but that!"

"I enjoyed his Beatles rendition much better," Evan said. "It seems we proved he has no tolerance for pain medication higher than a Tylenol."

"He's high," Kaden said.

"As a freaking kite," Sage added with a chuckle. He was perched on Kaden's lap since Kaden managed to grab one of the chairs.

Josh lifted his head and grinned. He tilted his head and stared straight at Evan. His eyes widened into saucer size. "Dude, I can see your aura. Man, it's bright."

His friends cracked up laughing.

"That's been his favorite one. He hit all of us with this aura stuff," Kaden said. "He went from dark and mysterious to bright white and pure. None of us are pure anything."

Moving closer to check Josh, Evan didn't know what to expect next. He was startled when Josh moved his right arm in a way to snag his doctor's coat and yank him down. His loopy, drunk patient—okay, potential boyfriend—planted a hot deep kiss on his mouth.

The band members whooped with joy and laughter. Some of them were so lost in their laughter they fell against one another wherever they found a way to sit in the small room. A couple found chairs while most grabbed a spot on the floor.

"Ahh. Much better," Josh said after the kiss. "Elevate me."

"Excuse me," Evan asked.

"Can't reach your lip-smacking goodness."

"I think you should stay right there."

"You helped me earlier. Why not now?" Josh pushed out his lower lip and trembled it.

"Crocodile tears are not gonna work." Evan stared down at his crazy patient. Sure enough, he found Josh's pupils wide, almost covering all of the dark green irises. "I agree with you guys, he's high as a kite."

"Yup. No hangover either. Yay." Josh snuggled against Doc's chest, as if petting him as he rubbed his face.

"We only see this side of him when he's completely smashed, but he barely drinks," Kaden said.

"Most of the time, he's the most straight-laced out of this obnoxious bunch," one of the men said from his place on the other chair. This one wore simple glasses over an elegant face, almost too feminine lines with high cheekbones and sharper jawline. His dark hair was slicked back, spiked in places, but ultra-fashion.

"Hey. You checking out my man, Thom—zhom—shom—" Grumbling how the words couldn't be formed, Josh stopped. "Shit. He's the techie geek."

"Learning everyone's faces since all of you outnumber me," Evan said, patting his fingers on Josh's shoulders.

"I'm Thomas Bellamy, the tech guy," Thomas said.

"Nice to meet all of you again," Evan said over Josh's off-key singing of a variety of verses.

"Wanna check out the lump under my gown, Doc? You can give me a spoooonge bath," Josh drawled.

His friends cracked up harder.

"Catheter, remember? Ouchie," Evan said.

Josh blew out a long raspberry. "No pain. I feel noooooo pain. Noooo pain."

"How long is this going to last?" Thomas asked.

"Until the medication works itself out of his brain and body. A couple of minutes to several hours. Does anyone know when the nurse came in?" Evan asked over Josh's random singing.

"A little after the dinner tray. About six?" Thomas said.

Evan checked the clock in the room. "So, perhaps another hour or so. He may nod off."

"Oooooh. Itch. Gotta itch...Itch...Help..." Josh wiggled his body on the bed.

Being the closest, Evan dropped his hand on Josh's covered thigh. "Don't wiggle so much. You'll dislodge something painful."

"Itch...itch...itch..."

"Where?"

"Hip. Scratch, please..." Josh pleaded.

Evan scratched in one spot, moving as Josh oooh and aahed and gave more directions.

"Oh yeah. That's it, Doc. Pleeease...Little higher...Left...Ahhh...There we go... Right there... Love ya—" Josh zonked out on them mid-sentence.

Evan realized the little bastard directed him until he was just above his crotch. "Joshua..." he said in a low tone.

Loud snores rumbled from Josh.

Evan shook his head as he stared at the knocked-out cowboy. "Such a lovable brat."

The rest of the band chuckled.

"Out like he got a knockout punch," Thomas said as he rose. "Hey, guys, let's get out of here and let our boy sleep. We'll tease him with all this blackmail shit another time."

With a grumble and groan, other members struggled to get to their feet from sitting on the floor. They all shook their limbs and did all kinds of weird stretches. A couple of them shared images and videos on their smart phones, obviously of everything that transpired in the room.

"We all shouldn't—" Sage started to protest.

"I'll stay with him," Evan said. "The recliner chair you're on can flatten into a bed. Not the best, but a flat place to sleep."

"You sure?"

Evan nodded. "I've had worse during my internships. Trust me. Go on. You guys have to get up with the sun to work the ranch. Plus, I know what to look for when he comes around."

"Thanks, Doc," Sage said, rising from Kaden's lap and hugged Evan.

Surprised at the embrace, Evan hugged back.

As Sage stepped back, Kaden stood and stretched. "Don't say it's all part of the job, this is more. Considered yourself adopted into our family. We take in all kinds of lost souls looking for a home." He patted Evan's shoulder.

Flushing light under the praise, Evan tucked his head down.

"We couldn't ask for anyone better for our Josh. He has a loving open heart and will take care of yours," Thomas said as he herded the other members out.

"We haven't—" Evan tried to protest.

"He has made his intentions known and we trust his decision. Night, Doc." Kaden waved a hand as they left the room.

Evan looked from the door, to the snoring man, and back. He left for a moment to head to the nurses' station.

"Got a little heavy in there," one nurse said with a chuckle.

"Hmm. No more strong pain medication for that man," Evan said. "However you can, flag the hell out of his records to warn everyone."

"I agree. Are you leaving, too?"

"No, I'm going to take advantage of his recliner. Can I get a pillow and couple of blankets?"

"Sure. I'll bring them to you."

"Appreciate it." Turning, Evan returned to the room. He removed his coat and hung it from a hook on back of the door. He pulled on the knot of the tie and loosened it completely. He bundled the silk length and shoved them in his coat pocket. After he unbuttoned his shirt and kicked off his shoes, he sat on the recliner. Using his weight, he stretched it out into the bed. Rising from it, he returned to Josh, checking on him.

"Here you go, Doc," the nurse said.

"Thanks." He escorted the nurse out, closed the door, and returned. He tossed the blankets and pillow on his makeshift bed. He yanked off his shirt and undid his pants to let them fall. Down to boxers, he gathered his clothes, folding them and placing them on a counter.

"Oooh. Hot damn, Doc. Didn't expect you to strip," Josh said, his words slurred with sleep and the meds.

Twisting around, Evan stared at him. "Were you faking that?"

"Nah, needed a nap," Josh said and yawned. "Looking sexy, Doc. Ya gonna join me?"

"Not in that bed, no. I'll take the recliner."

"Aww."

"You can't turn on your side in comfort, and I don't want you to knock yourself around again." Evan walked over to the bed. Bending over, he pressed his lips to Josh's lips, his cheeks, and ending at his temple. "Sleep."

"Always telling me to sleep. What's up with that?"

"Sleep heals. We can bring you home sooner."

"Still can't scratch my balls."

"Minor problem," Evan said with a chuckle. He tugged up the covers to tuck him in. He placed another kiss on Josh's mouth. "Sleep."

Closing his eyes before protesting, Josh slid back into sleep.

Shaking his head, Evan climbed on the recliner bed, shook out the pillows and punched the pillow a few times. Not what he expected, but after the day he had, he didn't want to be anywhere else. Hitting a switch to darken the room, he stretched out, covered himself with the blankets and turned to face Josh. Keeping Josh in his gaze, he let sleep roll over him like a gentle wave.

Two weeks later, Josh was in the uncomfortable, grumpy, and whiny phase of his recovery. The only bright spots were visits from the doctor to check on him and Miss Carolyn. They were brief appointments, so nothing could go further.

Miserable with his arms stuck stiff and out in front of him, Josh managed to grab a pen with his fingers and tapped it on the table. He was relegated to sit near Thomas, watching the rest of the band rehearse. He hated it. It made him feel worse sitting on the sidelines without his beloved violin in his hands.

He stared at the pen, twisting it up and down between his fingers.

It took some maneuvering and bending, but he managed to slide the pen under the cast and scratch at a few spots.

"Ahhhhhhhh," he said.

"Hey, stop that," Thomas said, smacking his hand and snatching the pen from him.

"I need that. I'm itchy as all hell in this heat," Josh whined.

"Joshua, you'll ruin the skin and cast. Knock it off," Thomas said, having received the most of Josh's complaints and whines.

"I'm bored as hell. I want my violin. I wanna be up there with the guys."

"I know. I know. Too damn bad. You need to heal."

"Heal, shmeal. This is taking forever."

Removing his glasses, Thomas rubbed at his temples.

"Hey, when did you get glasses?"

Thomas lifted his gaze and raised an eyebrow. "You're asking me that now?"

"What? All I got to do around here is to bug you."

"I got them a couple of days after the tour. Things were getting blurry on me." Thomas replaced the glasses and fiddled with the sound board to bring up the acoustic guitar.

"Blurry isn't good."

"Nope."

"Those frames look good on you."

Thomas gave him another glance and raised eyebrow.

"What? Just saying. You look good in them, stylish."

"Instead of dorky or complete geek?"

"You could pull off the dork look."

Thomas chuckled and shook his head.

"Why did we never hook up?"

"Tall, lean, and lanky isn't my type. We're better as friends," Thomas said. "Plus, you're not interested in the geek or nerd appearance. You enjoy your doctor's bod. Remember?"

"Oh please, that isn't right. You can't go wrong with me—ahh, the doc is perfect—" Josh trailed off with a sappy smile.

"It's all you get." Lifting his head, Thomas stared hard at Josh for a moment. "Oh no, please, don't get wishy washy on me."

"Who is your type?"

Dropping his gaze back on the board, Thomas shook his head once. "Not saying."

Josh narrowed his gaze on Thomas. "You already have someone. Don't you?"

"No. No, I don't."

"You gotta crush," Josh said in a sing-song kid's tone.

"Would you drop it?"

"No. I'm bored."

"You're worse than a kid on summer break."

Josh grinned and wiggled in his chair. He scratched his back on the desk.

"Hey!" Thomas rose and placed his hands on the different boards. "You're knocking around all the sensors. Stop that!"

"I'm itchy."

"You're being a whiny brat."

Josh pouted and settled back down in his chair.

"That's it. We're done." Thomas dropped back on his stool chair. He turned around and stared at Josh. "You need to go back to the house and take a nap."

"What? I'm not a child."

"Really?"

Josh closed his mouth.

"Hey? What's going on over there?" Sage asked them, using the microphone.

"Who's the next babysitter?" Thomas called out.

The band laughed.

"How long did it take, Josh?" one of them shouted.

Josh looked around at the clock. "Two hours and fifteen minutes. You owe me twenty-two bucks and fifty cents!"

"Shit," Arthur cursed and conferenced with others.

"What's with this cents shit?" Simon asked.

"For the fifteen minutes."

"What the—" Thomas looked from the stage to Josh and back. "Did you take a bet on me?"

"It's a bet on anyone to see how fast Josh can annoy the living hell out of them," the band member, Simon, said. "Ten dollars an hour. He's being a shit and breaking down the ten bucks for the minutes. If Josh wins, we each add the money to a jar. He'll get it when he gets free of the cast and can have fun."

"Shit," Thomas said.

Most of the band members laughed again. Harder this time.

"What happened this time?" Sage asked.

"He's treating me like a child," Josh snapped back.

"I'm sure you asked for it. Is he being whiny, cranky Josh again?" Sage asked.

"Yes, a cranky toddler who needs—" Thomas called back and gave Josh a daring look as if to argue against it. "A n-a-p!" He spelled out the last word to make his intention clear.

"I agree, Josh, go take a nap," Sage said.

Josh glared back and dropped his gaze to his feet. "Don't wanna. Tired of naps."

"You're cranky. You're whiny. I'm at the edge of wanting to smack you. Go. Take one of those pills the doc gave you and take a nap," Thomas said.

"We know you wanna be up here with us, man, but it's past time to quit with the whining right now," Simon said. "Even for the money, it's not funny."

"We're all with Simon. We want you here, too, but now isn't the time. We're just jamming up here, working on a few things. You're not missing out on much. We need you better and back on your feet," Sage said,

"Fine. Fine. Fine," Josh said as he struggled to stand. He adjusted his cast to hang better against his side. Turning, he stomped away from his friends and back to the house like a scolded child.

Having left the clinic once he finished adding notes to multiple patients' folders, Evan drove back to the ranch which held so much of his attention since his arrival in Montana. Parked in their lot, he grabbed his bag and tablet. His thumb brushed against something on the screen and activated the email. Pausing, Evan opened the inbox of his old email and pulled in a sharp breath.

Email after email. All of them from George. All of them nasty and harassing. All of them threatening him.

Not wanting to read any more, he canceled the entire account. The ones he wanted to speak with knew his current information. He wanted no connection to the bastard he left in Texas. It wasn't worth his time or the stress level.

There was someone here who could take far better care with his heart. He wanted to give it the chance their connection deserved.

Turning off the tablet, he shoved it back in his bag. He grabbed it and his medical kit and left the car. Hearing music, he paused to listen to it, smiling at the great beat.

"Hey there, Doc. How ya doing?" Charlie asked as he walked away from a corral where a cowboy worked a young horse on a long lead.

"You're always around whenever I appear," Evan said with a smile.

"It's my job to oversee everything for the boys along with all kinds of other things."

"They sound real good."

"Even better with Josh sawing away on his fiddle."

"Hopefully we'll get him back there soon. How is Miss Carolyn doing?"

"She's holding her own, but not talking as much. Sleeping a lot. Your uncle was here earlier to check on her vitals and pain level. He doesn't suspect she'll last another month."

"Will her oldest son be able to arrive home in time?"

"We're still waiting for contact from Basil or his chain of command. Things remain broken with the family, and I'm not sure if he wants to speak with anyone in the family. It's a sad outcome. Basil broke all ties after his argument with his daddy and he joined the Marines. It wasn't the best of partings."

"I hope you find him." Evan looked around. "Where is Josh? Is he with the others?"

"No, they kicked his ass out. He went upstairs for a forced nap," Charlie said with a chuckle. "Go on up and see him."

"Thanks, appreciate the update." Evan entered the house. He stepped out of his dusty boots as required by the residents.

"Is that you, Doc Evan? How are you?" Loretta asked. "Can I get you anything?"

Exchanging a few words with Loretta, Evan jogged upstairs and headed to Josh's bedroom. Since the door was partially opened, he pushed it open and stepped inside.

Upon the bed, his chest bare to the two rotating fans circulating the air, Josh reclined on the bed. His eyes were closed. Pillows propped and supported both of his arms. Due to the heat of the day, his chest was slicked with sweat, and his hair was darker around his forehead.

Taking a chance, Evan closed the bedroom door to a crack. After setting his bags on the dresser, he stripped out of the white coat and yanked off his tie. Around this family, he could let down most of the doctor façade. They accepted him for who he was. It was something he enjoyed and wished for more. Moving to the bed, he settled on the edge.

What was it about this lanky cowboy that cracked the shell around his heart after the disaster with George? Of course, Josh was absolutely nothing like George. He wasn't an egomaniac. He cared more about his band members, now his closest family, than himself. Evan could tell this from Josh's injury. He wondered how long Josh played in pain so he wouldn't let the band down.

Reaching out with his closest hand, Evan traced one damp curl of hair and slid it off Josh's forehead.

Startled, his breath hitched a bit, as Josh opened his eyes. A slow smile curled his lips as his gaze brightened. "Doc, I was dreaming about you."

"Was it a good dream?"

"Oh, yeah, I didn't want to leave it, but now I have you in the flesh, so to speak." Josh waggled his eyebrows. "You've been making a lot of house calls for little ole me."

"I wanted to keep a close watch over my favorite patient."

"Favorite, huh?"

Evan chuckled as he pushed another curl from Josh's forehead and tucked it behind his ear. "Yes, a favorite of mine. Though I shouldn't even think about you in any way other than a patient, but—" He shrugged.

"We can scoot around regulations around here. No one will report you to a board or anything. Our secret is safe," Josh said with a slow wink. "Whatcha here for this time?"

"I want to check out your arms. Lucas called and wanted me to check on how you were healing. I spoke with the orthopedic, and we can remove part of the cast to look at the stitches. If your skin is closed, I can remove the stitches."

"What if they're not healed?"

"I'll remove the rest of the cast and fit a new one around your hand and wrist. I can use cotton and Ace bandages around the rest of the injuries. Either way, you should have a bit more freedom."

"Oh, please do. It's hard to get dressed, go to the bathroom, and even a decent shower. I crave a shower. I hate relying on Miss Loretta to help me."

"We need to remain cautious and careful. One slip-up, and it could be more surgery or the end of your musical career."

"That would suck."

With a nod of agreement, Evan grabbed his medical bag. He walked around the bed to reach Josh's right arm. Tugging on blue sterile gloves, he used small scissors to snip the white bandage off. He unrolled the rest and tossed all of it in a red medical waste bag. He gently took hold of Josh's arm, turning it slightly to check out the healing incision. They both looked at the incision from the inside of Josh's biceps to mid-forearm below the elbow.

Josh grimaced. "Hell, that's a long one."

"It's what Lucas needed to get access to your nerve. The same incision is on your other arm."

Josh looked down and then back at Evan. "How well do you know Lucas?"

Evan paused as he pulled out the instruments to cut the threads. "Pardon?"

"You talk about him like he's a good friend. I noticed it before when you were conferencing. You guys dropped all the usual doctor pretense."

"You noticed?"

"Yeah."

"He's my best friend and helped me out of a bad situation."

"Back in Texas?"

"Yes, he's one of the few I could count on for support and complete confidentiality. Hold your arm still. I'm going to snip these stitches free." Evan hooked the first stitch and snipped it.

"Were you hurt somehow? You told me you were broken. How?"

Evan lifted his gaze to look at Josh and dropped back as he snipped another thread. "Yes. I was in a relationship and it went sour."

"Did he hurt you?"

"There was abuse."

"Oh, shit, Doc," Josh said.

When Evan glanced up, he saw Josh's eyes were brimmed with tears and shiny with anger. His heart clenched at the thought of Josh coming to his support and rescue.

Josh shook his head once. "No one should ever go through that shit. Are you afraid to try again?"

"Are you offering?"

"Yeah, I guess I am."

Evan glanced up before he clipped again. "Not because I'm the new fish in town."

"No, something else is there. Come on, Doc, you know we hit it off."

"A couple of sparks. You can call me Evan."

"Don't like Doc?"

"Not when we're in bed. I'm not a doctor then," Evan said and continued to snip. It took a few more minutes, but soon all of the stitches were removed. "Looks like Lucas used both the stitches and glue to seal you up."

"Will it scar?"

Evan checked out the reddened line. "It'll be noticeable but not thick. Just a long white line, but I recommend using Vitamin E oil to help it heal but only after full closure happens." Rising, Evan went to the bathroom, soaked a washcloth in warm water and grabbed a hand towel. He returned to the bed and wiped down Josh's arm with the cloth and dried it. "Keep the wound clean and dry for the next couple of weeks." Setting the cloths aside, Evan pulled out a stack of long adhesive bandages. He used several to cover the length of the wound. "Use these bandages only, but use warm water to release the glue. Don't peel. Your skin regains its tensile strength slowly, so protect it from any further injury for another month. Keep your arms covered by a shirt from the sun and dust."

Finishing with the right arm, he brought his bag and the cloths to the other side of the bed. Lifting the casted arm, he touched the fingertips, asked Josh a couple of questions, and made sure Josh wiggled his fingers.

"Looks like your family went to town on the cast," Evan said, tapping several colorful areas.

"Yeah, they broke out a rainbow collection of Sharpies and went crazy. I don't mind. Better than the plain white," Josh said with a grin.

"Has there been any pain or swelling?"

"A little the first week, but I used the ice pack like you said. A little more on the achy pain end of things, so I take the ibuprofen you gave me."

Lifting his hands, Evan checked where the edge of the cast wrapped around the shoulder. He noticed the skin was a little irritated and bruised but not much. "Are you using a sling?"

"Sometimes. It's more of an annoyance because of the positioning."

"True, but it'll help relieve some pressure from your neck."

"When am I getting rid of it?"

"Since your other arm healed nicely, I'm going to remove the upper part of the cast today. I'll cut it down to below the elbow. Your hand and wrist will still be supported, but it will give you some mobility."

"I'll do whatever you tell me, if you give me the ability to shower and dress on my own."

Chuckling, Evan pulled the specialized cast saw from his bag. He plugged it into the outlet.

"Ooh. You brought the clinic to me," Josh said.

"According to my uncle, it's all part of the job of creating a mobile clinic, but I'm also giving you some special attention."

"Aww. You *weally weally* like me," Josh said in a teasing tone. "What else is in that magic bag? Are you going to pull out a tall floor lamp next?"

Evan chuckled. "Nothing like Mary Poppins' carpet bag, but all kinds of good stuff." Rising again, he returned to the bathroom and found a large bath towel. Shaking it out, he walked back to the bed. Removing the stacked pillows, he laid out the arm on the towel, helping Josh lay flat on the bed in the process. "Okay. I need you to hold still."

"I've had a couple of these in my lifetime as a crazy kid and working as a cowboy. I remember the sensation and process."

Evan placed a surgical mask in place to protect him from any dust. With a black Sharpie, he marked the cuts he wanted to make on the cast. "Hold still."

Starting the small vibrating saw, Evan cut into the thick plaster. He sliced down both sides and a couple of half circles below the elbow. Using another tool, he pried open the cast on either side. He pulled off one upper half and then the second side. With scissors, he cut through the layers of cotton padding and stockinette. Soon, he revealed the pale skin of Josh's arm.

Grabbing the damp cloth, he wiped the scaly skin, removing layers of dead skin, and cleaned the area. He dried it off with the towel and removed the mask.

"Ick. Looks all wrinkly and nasty," Josh complained, and when Evan gently turned his arm, he murmured, "Ouch..."

Holding still, Evan glanced at Josh. "What? What is it?"

"Elbow and shoulder are stiff."

"Sorry, I forgot. They've been held in one position for a while." Evan gently massaged both joints with his fingers. "Let me remove and bandage the sutures, and we'll be good."

Almost another half hour later, Evan finished with both of Josh's arms. He cleaned up all the medical waste, adding everything to the red bag he'd toss out at the clinic. He double-checked the remaining cast.

He placed his hand on the smaller cast and glanced at Josh's face. "This will stay on for another three weeks. If it becomes loose and wiggly, call me or come to the clinic. I'll need to recast it to maintain the stability of the break."

"Understand. Otherwise, same type of care?"

"Yes. Cover the cast tight with a plastic bag before you go near a shower or any water."

"I know. Ahh, a shower all by myself. Yay!"

With a smile Evan packed up the rest of his kit.

"Are you leaving?" Josh asked, sitting straighter in the bed and gently tested and rolled his shoulder.

"You were my last appointment of the day. I can head back home."

"What's home?"

"The little cabin behind the clinic."

Josh licked his lower lip. "Don't leave. Stay here with me. Please. For dinner, for laughs, and...for us. Will you stay?"

Taking the chance to see where things would go, Evan gave him a nod. "It would be my honor."

Josh's smile warmed the deepest, guarded parts of Evan's heart. "Good. Then get up and lock the door for us, Doc."

Realizing where Josh was taking this between them, Evan tossed aside all the internal fight of being with a patient. As Josh said, they were both adults and nowhere near anyone who would report them or even think about it. Rising from the bed, Evan gathered all of his medical things and placed them on the floor not far from the door. He closed the door and locked it.

Turning, he saw Josh make a "come here" motion with his fingers.

Grinning, Evan unbuttoned the once-starched, pale blue shirt, now wrinkled from the heat of the day. Letting the shirt fall to the floor, as he walked back, he unbuckled his belt and worked slowly on the pants. After another step, he let the pants drop, weighed down by the belt. He took the last few steps in plain socks and white boxer briefs.

"Hmm, like the choice of underwear, Doc," Josh said with a waggle of his eyebrows.

"Less chafing in this heat. I prefer regular boxers," Evan said, dropping on the bed. He bent and yanked off the socks.

Josh used his right hand to whip back the sheet and reveal his pair of striped boxers. "Only thing I can step into on my own. I really didn't want anyone to help me get in and out of my undershorts."

Evan chuckled. "Now you'll have a little more freedom in your attire."

Josh held up his hand to Evan. "Come and cuddle. I want more of those delicious kisses."

Stretching out under the covers, Evan slid up against Josh. As he turned them, he tugged Josh into his arms and held him against his chest, supporting him. "Looks like I better do most of the work."

"Would be best this time around," Josh said and tilted his head.

Evan kissed his impatient cowboy a little, lips only brushing and pressing against one another. He teased those lush lips apart a bit at a time with sweeps of his tongue. Each time, he dipped further, as if seeking something richer, deeper inside Josh.

As he slid his tongue in and met Josh's, the thrill of kissing this man dropped straight to his cock, hard and aching against the compression of the cotton briefs. He kept the kiss to only their mouths and tongues. He used his hands only to hold Josh close in place against him, one of his hands cupped the back of Josh's head.

In time, as the soft moans increased, he removed the one hand from Josh's head and slowly made his way down the lithe frame of his cowboy. He trailed his fingers along the spine, finding the dimples at the base and slid underneath the band of the boxers. There he found the glory of the hard globes of Josh's ass. Squeezing one of those cheeks, knowing they were built from hours sitting in the saddle, he teased the heated crack between with a single finger.

Josh's moans increased as he shivered against him. He clenched his ass cheeks around Evan's finger. Josh rolled them, wiggling until the touch of his cotton-covered hard cock glided along Evan's own covered cock.

Evan moved his hand to hold Josh's hips, swiveling and circling his hips to press their cocks closer, using the cotton to heighten the desire and sensations. He continued to capture Josh's soft noises within his kisses.

Again and again, they continued to kiss, sweet, teasing, and heated.

"More, please," Josh whispered.

Rolling them again until Josh was on his back, Evan slid between Josh's thighs, opening them. He never stopped his kisses.

Soft wordless sounds left Josh as Evan moved his hands over Josh's body, touching him, finding those secret spots to make Josh wiggle and moan. He slid his fingers between Josh's sweat-damp belly and the boxer's waistband.

Josh gasped against Evan's mouth. "Off. Want them off. Please."

"Soon. Promise," Evan said.

Breaking the delicious string of kisses, he trailed kisses and nips from Josh's mouth, chin, down the column of his throat, and lapped at both collarbones. He followed another path across Josh's chest, tasting every part he touched earlier. He found Josh adored having his nipples sucked hard with a few tender bites.

"Oh, sweet Jesus, shit..."Josh cried out as his body arched with the sensation. "Could come just from that."

"You're young. I'll get you back up there," Evan teased.

"Not filling my damn shorts like a kid."

Even with that determined tone, Evan didn't let up on those flat brown nipples. He brought his fingers into play, tweaking the nipple he wasn't attached to. He moved his thigh between Josh's legs, opening them wider until he nudged the thick erection pressing against the cotton boxers.

With all of these sensations flooding his systems, Josh cursed Evan as he drove higher. He groaned hard as his cock shot his cum into his boxers, filling them. "Sonofa—" Josh cursed, his voice breathless as his body shuddered from the hard release.

"Ready for more?" Evan said, lifting his head from Josh's chest to study his flushed face.

"Oh God, please. I want you to fill me, Evan."

"Will be my pleasure, eventually," Evan said.

Not pausing this time, Evan kissed down Josh's abdomen, licking along the edge of the waist band. Lifting his head, he breathed in the scents of musk, sweat, and recent spent cum. A damp stain increased across the front of Josh's boxers.

"Tsk. Tsk. Such a mess. Shall have to clean this," Evan said. Pushing himself up, he made quick work of stripping both of their undershorts. He dropped them to the floor and stared down at what he revealed.

Even with the recent release, Josh's cock was long and thick, curving toward his belly as arousal washed over his body. The purpling shaft glistened as new droplets of clear fluid dripped from the head. His cock rested against a nest of thick, dark curls matching the caramel-shaded hair on his head.

Trembling at the sight of his lover's body, Evan licked away the streaks of Josh's seed from the abdomen and hips. He enjoyed the salty sweetness of Josh's cum and wanted more of it. Rising to his knees, he grasped the base with his fingers and cleaned the glistening shaft with more licks as if he enjoyed a frozen Popsicle.

Josh gripped the sheet with his right hand as his hips rolled, restless against Evan's touch. All kinds of delightful noises left him.

Releasing the shaft, Evan watched it lower back to Josh's body. He nuzzled those wiry curls with his nose, breathing in the scents that made up Josh, and teased the edges with his tongue. Again, Josh lifted his hips with an urgency for more as he cried out with a plea.

The lovely sac underneath the shaft was covered in golden skin, soft and wrinkly. Evan played with them, teasing them with his nose and tongue. Then he licked and kissed his way back up the long shaft, knowing one night he would have the thick length filling his ass, and lapped at the droplets of fluid. Lifting his head, he watched the plum-colored head moisten as it wept drop after drop. Licking his mouth in anticipation of taking it deep inside, Evan waited and blew warm breaths along the moist skin watching Josh shudder and react.

Holding Josh's thighs down with his hands, Evan wrapped his mouth over the flared head. Teasing as long as he could, feeling his own sac tighten and his cock bobbing, aching for attention, he flicked his tongue along the slit and the sweet bundle of nerves under the blunt head.

Tormenting both of them, Evan lingered on the flared head. He licked around the edge. He played with the amount of suction until Josh gasped, cursed, and pleaded in sharper tones. Taking the plunge, he sank down on the rigid shaft, swirling his tongue around the vein ridges. Shoving his hands under Josh's hips, he cupped the fine ass and lifted him, suckling the rest of the girth. He felt the hard nudge at the back of his throat and swallowed deep.

Josh sank the fingers of his good hand in Evan's hair and shouted, trying to fight another release. His body quivered like a tightly strung bow, arching under Evan's touch.

Evan swallowed again, rose to let himself breath, and sank again.

With a third swallow, Josh let out a choked cry. It was Evan's only warning before the shaft went harder. The slit released one jet after another down his throat. His mouth flooded with Josh's salty taste, and he swallowed every drop. If he could, he would have let out a cry of his own as his cock shot against the sheets.

As the flood finished, Evan sucked, swirled, and stroked the shaft clean with his mouth and tongue. While he let go of Josh's ass, he released the flared head with a satisfying pop of suction. Licking his reddened lips, Evan stretched forward and captured Josh's mouth, sharing the taste with him.

He dropped to Josh's side, trailing his fingers down the dark caramel curls bisecting his abdomen. Josh's body glistened with sweat. The thick spent shaft against his thigh. His abdomen rose and fell with every gasp of breath.

"Holy... shit..."Josh managed as he turned to stare at Evan. His eyes dark, unsteady. Beads of sweat rolled around his face, darkening his hair.

Letting lazy kisses and desire linger for a little longer, the dual fans continued to send long sweeps of swirled air around them. They dispelled and stirred the scents of seed and sex within the room. Evan knew he hadn't had enough of his cowboy. He wanted more. He wanted to claim this man as his.

"Ready for another round?" he asked, wrapping his hand around Josh's shaft, giving it a long swirling stroke.

Josh groaned as his hips rose to the grasp. "Gonna kill me."

"We'll die together. Smiles across our faces. Our balls completely drained. A good death."

"Death by pleasure. Hell, yes." Tilting his head, Josh accepted deeper kisses from Evan, heating things up once more.

There was something to be taken care of between them, and Evan rose back to a kneeling position. He kept his grip on Josh's shaft. "Condom? Lube?"

"Top drawer," Josh said with a wave of his casted hand toward the nightstand. "I'm clean."

"I know. I saw your tests." Releasing the silken shaft, Evan stretched out to open the drawer. He found the tube of lube and box of foiled packets.

"You?"

Evan paused as he picked up a condom. "I'm clean, too. I took a test before leaving Texas to make sure the bastard didn't give me anything. He drank a lot and didn't give a shit who was in his bed or where he stuck his cock."

"Doc, I don't want to hear about him in our bed. He's no longer part of your life." Josh curled his good hand around Evan's cheek. "As for us, I don't want anyone else in my bed now or at any future time. Skin to skin. Flood me with your seed and scent. Make me yours." His gaze brightened with sexual need and desire.

"I had that once. It went bad."

"That was with a bastard in Texas. He's not here."

"No. No he's not here anymore."

"Good, remember that. This is with me. I never cheated, not once since I knew I wanted a man in my life. I had one partner at a time, always with protection. I'm done searching. My heart wants you."

Tossing the lube between his hands, Evan stared down at Josh, listening to those promises.

"It's not the arousal or sex talking. Take me."

Flicking the packet back into the drawer, Evan closed it without keeping one. He slid back toward Josh.

"Damn, this is gonna feel like heaven," Josh said in a reverent whisper. "Like this. Face to face."

"Need to help you in a better position. Again, I'll do the work." Evan smiled as he grabbed a couple of pillows and stuffed them under Josh's hips, raising his ass in a better position. He tucked the others behind Josh's head and shoulders to support him and allow the cowboy to watch him.

As Evan moved into position again, Josh happily opened his legs wider and tilted his knees back. The sexual position revealed the tight, puckered entrance to Evan.

Kneeling between Josh's thighs, Evan stroked his cock a couple of times. The shaft hardened as he studied the hole he would enter. Licking his lips, he squeezed a generous amount of lube on his palm and spread it on his shaft and head.

Adding more lube to his fingers, he set the tube aside. He slid his finger along the taint from the dark sac to the entrance. He circled around the ring, teasing it, loosening it. He slipped a finger through the taut ring and heard Josh's moan with his body's first stretch. On either side, Evan watched Josh's powerful thigh muscles go taut under the golden skin.

"Has it been a while?" Evan asked.

"Yeah. Over a year."

"I'll take care of you."

Evan pumped his single finger, hooking around the ring before a few more pumps. Drawing out the gentle preparation, he slipped in additional fingers one at a time. Each time, he worked and pumped them deeper. He curled his fingers and pressed against the spot inside Josh.

He continued to tease and rake his fingers against the spot until Josh's toes curled. He watched Josh bang his fist against the bed. Curses and pleas left him. His breathing caught and fell in harsher breaths.

"Please. Enough. No more. Please. I crave you. I'm stretched," Josh said as he met Evan's gaze, his pupils blown from pleasure as Josh worked the gland.

Pulling his fingers out, Evan bent over and kissed Josh for several moments. He grasped his cock and held the head against the prepared opening. Staring deep into Josh's eyes, he pressed forward and penetrated his lover.

"Oh, fuck, so damn good." Josh tilted his head back on the pillows and moaned as his body opened to the gentle invasion.

"Breathe, baby, push back against me," Evan encouraged as he sat up and watched Josh accept his cock.

Blowing out a deliberate breath, Josh tilted and pushed back against Evan.

"Watch us come together, baby," Evan said as he yanked a pillow from Josh's hips.

Josh curled forward and stared as his ring stretched around Evan. "Holy hell, you're so damn thick and long." He licked his lips and laid back. He raised both hands across his face as he moaned. His cast hung heavy on one side.

Evan pumped the flared head of his cock inside a few times, encouraging Josh's body to relax around him. He closed his eyes for a moment, concentrating on the intense heat surrounding him. If it was this hot for him, he figured it felt like fire racing through Josh's body.

"More. Do it. Feed your cock into me," Josh said. "Do it."

With gentle, steady rolls of his hips, Evan moved inch by thicker inch into Josh's entrance. He braced himself with a hand on the bed near Josh's hip. He used his other hand to steady Josh's hips. "Easy. Don't rock too hard, or you'll dislodge me. We'll have to start all over."

Josh moaned, as if wanting that.

"As you wish, my lover," Evan said and pulled completely out, his cock hating the cold after the fiery heat. He slid his fingers back into the greedy hole, raking the spot again.

Josh shouted all kinds of curses at Evan.

Using his other hand, Evan cupped the base of his shaft and tapped the head several times against Josh's sac and entrance. "Hold still like a good boy," Evan teased as he guided his cock back inside. He moaned when Josh's ring squeezed around the flared head, teasing the bundle of nerves and making Evan's eyes cross with pleasure. "Oh shit, right there. So good."

"Do it! Shove yourself in! No more teasing."

Knowing Josh's body was ready, Evan clamped both hands on Josh's hips and penetrated deep inside Josh.

Josh sucked in a breath through clenched teeth and let out a long, low groan at the harsh slide of flesh. He lowered his knees, letting his feet fall near Evan's thighs, keeping him close. "More...Take me. Use me."

With a slow pace, Evan found a rhythm to suit them, moving his thick cock in and out until he heard his sac slapping Josh's flesh. He altered the strokes with speed, depth, and strength. He lifted one of Josh's legs, raising it with the crook of his elbow to adjust the tilt to make sure to peg that gland.

Josh undulated and moaned around him as he came alive around him. "Full... So damn full and stretched. Do it! Fuck me!"

Planting one hand on the bed, Evan jerked his hips, circled, and slammed. Over. And over. Again. And again.

Burying his cock over and over into Josh's heat, he glided over the perfect spot, firing pleasure straight to the gland. Josh's body arched and undulated harder underneath him as he continued to peg that gland. Pushing Josh's leg to curl high around his back, he planted his other hand on the bed for better counterweight. Using it, he slammed and buried himself until the bed rocked with their motions, the headboard hitting the wall in the same rhythmic pattern.

Sweat slicked across his forehead, falling into his eyes, but Evan didn't stop. He couldn't leave the fiery heat of this intimate embrace of flesh to flesh. Deep inside Josh's body, feeling it clench around him.

Until Evan lost control. He leaned forward, murmuring unknown words against Josh, each thrust, each pounding harder than the one before, each drive deeper, less controlled. He felt his sac tighten. "You there—"

"Fuck—"

Evan straightened and froze, his body trembling against Josh. He held Josh's hips tighter, his fingers digging into the golden skin slick with sweat. His hips continued their furious rock and pumping.

Josh squeezed his tender ring around Evan's cock. His legs locked around Evan, his ankle dug into Evan's back. He groaned loudly, his release triggering everything. His cock released without even being touched, seed splashing across his belly. Some even shot up toward his chest.

Evan felt the fire race down his spine and cried out Josh's name. He sent the first spray of cum deep inside Josh's body. He coated his lover deep inside with multiple shots. He had never come so fucking hard in his entire life.

Josh's inner muscles clamped around him, squeezing every bit of cum from his tender cock. Evan couldn't help himself but responded with a few jerky thrusts of his hips, adding to the storm building between him. Josh gave another wordless cry as he went through a dry orgasm, triggering the same from Evan.

"Fuck...Fuck...Shit..." Josh cursed as his body spiraled out of control with the orgasms.

Evan wanted to say the same, but the pleasure crossed his eyes and kept all words from him.

When the storm of pleasure washed over them, Evan slid his limp cock from Josh's hole. Josh's legs dropped to the bed, freeing Evan from their grip. Evan managed to drop hard to the bed on Josh's right side, utterly exhausted from the experience. He let his limbs sprawl across Josh's longer body. He wasn't sure if he would ever move again. Not even his eyes wanted to open. The only thing he could do was concentrate on his breathing.

Feeling the mattress move, he opened his eyes and locked with Josh's gaze. A lazy smile curled the cowboy's lips. They both let out soft laughter, sated beyond belief.

"Holy shit, what the hell was that?" Evan whispered, his voice rough from the cries.

"Don't know, but I want it again."

More laughter between them.

"Greedy bastard," he teased his cowboy. Dragging his aching body, he curled around Josh, enclosing him within his limbs, nuzzled the back of his neck, and let exhaustion and sleep take over.

Chapter Eleven

After that sensual night, Evan wasn't far from Josh's side or the ranch. With the blessings and teasing of the others, he gradually moved his things into Josh's room. He enjoyed seeing his business-like shirts and pants hanging near denim worn from time and use.

When he wasn't on call and sleeping alone in the small cabin by the clinic, Evan returned to the ranch every night. He laughed over the dinner table with the others, sharing tender glances with Josh. Late into the evenings, they touched and made their bodies dance and shiver with intense pleasure.

The only thing interrupting his happiness was a call from Texas. Luckily, the caller was Lucas with news. George had been arrested for disorderly conduct after arriving drunk for a surgery and a charge of murder or something else when his patient died. Lucas wasn't fully aware of the extent of charges, but George's career and freedom were gone. The family of the patient filed another suit against him for malpractice when he let the patient die under his shaky knife. With the knowledge that George would never be leaving prison, the last bands of fear and uncertainty released their grip on Evan's heart.

Free. He was completely free from his past.

Evan felt lighter than the clouds.

Lingering over the ranch like a dark cloud was how Miss Carolyn continued to linger in the cabin. She kept fighting against the cancer ravaging her body. Evan wondered if she waited for her oldest son, Basil, to return home, or if she wanted her husband to come to the cabin.

Either way, the watch over her continued.

Several weeks later, Evan removed the remainder of Josh's cast, gave him an ACE bandage and instructions to go slow. It was another thing he could watch while spending time with Josh. Josh laughed and almost preened under the attention.

Evan wandered into the musical barn one late afternoon, following the music. Still unable to practice and jam with the others, Josh stood near Thomas' area, braced against a pole, one boot crossed over and tapping to the rhythm of the bass guitar and drums.

With a smile Evan walked up behind him, pressed a light kiss against the base of Josh's neck, and wrapped his arms around his lean cowboy.

Startled by Evan's sneak attack, Josh's body shuddered under his touch but settled back against him. Evan linked his hands around Josh's belly, felt one calloused hand pressed against his hands.

"Hey there, cowboy," he whispered into Josh's ear, nipping the earlobe.

Josh wiggled under the sensual assault and turned to stare at him. "What's up, Doc?" He waggled his eyebrows as he drawled his favorite saying.

Evan chuckled and squeezed him. "Off early."

"Sweet."

"What are they playing?"

"Some of the newer tunes to lay down the notes to the lyrics Sage worked on the last month. I'll add the fiddle in when I can play," Josh said and explained what the band was doing in low tones.

As the song wrapped up with Sage's acceptance over the arrangements, the band finished the session. Next to them, Thomas turned his stool around as others called out hellos to Evan.

"Do you know how to play something, Doc?" Thomas asked with a smile.

"Trained in piano as a kid," Evan admitted.

"Want a turn?"

"I don't know. It's been a while since I played anything," Evan said.

Andrew, the keyboardist and piano player, waved Evan over. "Come on and give it a try, Doc. No one judges around here."

Releasing his grip around Josh, Evan glanced at him. "Do you mind?"

"Nah. Go ahead. I wanna see your other skills. I'll sit with you," Josh said and whispered in Evan's ear, "You play my body just fine. Let's see what else you can play with those talented fingers."

Evan removed his light jacket and tie. He handed both to Thomas. While following Josh toward the low stage, he unbuttoned the sleeves and rolled them up. He fist bumped Andrew and settled on the bench. Staring down at the black and white keys, he blew out a long breath.

"Show us what you have, Doc. We'll join in," Sage said with a smile of encouragement.

Testing a few keys with his fingers, watching memory muscle return to them, Evan tapped out a simple melody. Josh sat on the bench next to him, watching. "Okay. Let's see if I remember this..."

Counting low to himself, Evan placed his hands on the keys and played the opening notes to Garth Brooks' "*The Dance*". Singing the lyrics low, Evan looked over at Josh, seeing his eyes widen in surprise.

"You sing, too?" Josh asked.

The guys hooted and hollered with joy, taking up their instruments and joining the beautiful ballad. With Evan taking the lyrics, Sage picked up one of his guitars and slung the strap over his shoulder.

"Louder, Doc," Andrew encouraged as he moved the microphone.

Evan's rich tones flowed through the microphone, singing the sweet, sad lyrics Garth created. Sage, Arthur, Randall, and Simon joined in as back-up vocals, merging the harmonies with ease.

Still, Evan continued to sing to Josh. He slid easily from "*The Dance*" to Rascal Flatts' "*Bless the Broken Road*" to "*Please Remember*

Me" by Tim McGraw and ended with Brad Paisley's loving "*Then*". He changed "girl" to "boy" as he met Josh's gaze. Josh joined in the choruses as Sage tried to match Paisley's brilliance on the guitar.

Finishing the impromptu jam session, Evan lowered his hands and smiled. He realized he missed playing music.

Rocked to the side, Josh embraced him hard enough they almost fell off the bench. As the music lifted, he heard the rest of the band cheering and whistling in appreciation.

"It's cemented. You're never, ever leaving me," Josh said, staring straight into Evan's gaze.

Evan whispered the last lyric of "Then" to Josh, ending with, "I loved you..." Thought not required by the song, he paused and stared at Josh. "Then."

The End

Dreamy...Sensual...Forever Love

A quiet one, Nicole Dennis is the penname of an asexual author of different genres of fiction – both LGBT+ and hetero. Lots of characters, worlds, and stories build up in her head until she must get them down on the screen – anything from romance to fantasy to paranormal.

During the day, she works in a quiet office in Central Florida, where she makes her home, and enjoys the down time to slip into her imagination. She is owned by a feline companion – a fluffy house panther, known as Midnight the Void. A very special furbaby who is FIV+ and polydactyl on her front paws (fluffy danger mittens!).

Contact & Media Info

Website: http://nicoledennis.net
Email: nicoledennis.author@gmail.com
Facebook:

Main: www.facebook.com/NicoleDennis.Author
Page: https://www.facebook.com/NicoleDennis.Musings/
Group: https://www.facebook.com/groups/nicoledennis.author/

Amazon: https://www.amazon.com/author/nicoledennis
Threads: https://www.threads.net/@ndennis_author
Mastodon: https://mastodon.lol/@nicoledennis
QueeRomance: https://www.queeromanceink.com/mbm-book-author/nicole-dennis/
Goodreads: http://www.goodreads.com/author/show/2791975.Nicole_Dennis

Pride Publishing
Southern Charm Series

1 – Rules of the Chef
2 – By the Numbers
3 – On the Green
4 – When in Bloom
5 – Following the Law
6 – According to Design
7 – Unexpected in the End (Coming 2025)
Freebies available on my website or email for PDF

Mischief Corner Books:
Secrets & Silk
Siren Publishing: (BookStrand.com)
Grant's Mechanic (MM)
Unholy Angel (MF Erotic Paranormal)
Fire Jaguars (MMF Paranormal)

1 – Fire Moon Dance
2 – Luna Moon Dance
3 – Dark Moon Dance
Other books are in the works

FatCat Books Ink (Self-Pub home):
New Stories:
Lyon Lynx Clan

Paws in the Snow (Prequel)

McShayne Bloodline

1 – McShayne's Dragon
2 – McShayne's Fae
3 – McShayne's Elf
4 – McShayne's Merman (Coming 2025)

Cheimon Tales

1 – Cracks in the Ice
2 – Strike's Stand (In the works)
3 – Mistletoe's Story (In the works)

Carnival of Mysteries (Multi-Author Collection)

1 – Dryad on Fire
2 – Flames of the Arcane

Re-Releases:
Walk Me Trilogy

1 – Walk Me Down the Middle
2 – Walk Me Through the Haze
3 – Walk Me Through the Darkness

7 Days of Christmas
Built Piece by Piece
At the Masquerade

www.ingramcontent.com/pod-product-compliance
Lightning Source LLC
Chambersburg PA
CBHW031424150726

47989CB00002B/781